There was only one thing Karen was certain about: She sure was glad she'd fallen in love with this man!

"It must have been rather sudden," she said to Jack.

He nodded. "Love at first sight."

"I guess!" she said, studying his face. She could see how it might have happened. He had a nice face, boyish but just imperfect enough to be interesting as well as masculine and definitely handsome.

Still, it seemed so unlike her. She had a feeling she hadn't been acting herself lately.

But what made her believe him was the electricity she felt sparking between them, especially when their gazes met and held.

Like right now. He'd looked over at her, concern still in the depths of his brown eyes. She felt herself sizzle under his gaze and smiled shyly. They must have a great sex life. She couldn't wait to have her memory refreshed....

Dear Harlequin Intrigue Reader,

Chills run down your spine, your pulse pounds...and you can't wait to turn the page! It's just another month of outstanding romantic suspense from Harlequin Intrigue.

Last month, Amanda Stevens introduced you to a new brand of justice—GALLAGHER JUSTICE—in *The Littlest Witness* (#549). This month, Detective Tony Gallagher gets his very own *Secret Admirer* (#553) for Valentine's Day. Cupid is also hard at work in B.J. Daniels's *Love at First Sight* (#555), in which a sexy police officer has to pose as the husband of the only witness to a murder in order to protect her. Except he keeps forgetting their marriage is supposed to be a façade.

Caroline Burnes takes a break from her FEAR FAMILIAR series to bring you *Texas Midnight* (#554). Simmering passion and a remote location make for an explosive read from this bestselling author. But Familiar, the crime-solving black cat, will be back at Harlequin Intrigue soon in his *thirteenth* novel! Watch for *Familiar Obsession* (#570) in stores this June.

Finally, Rita Herron contributes to the ongoing Harlequin Intrigue amnesia promotion A MEMORY AWAY... with *Forgotten Lullaby* (#556). In this highly emotional story, not only do a man and woman commit their love to one another once, but they also overcome the odds to fall in love all over again.

Intense drama and powerful romance make for an extraspecial selection of titles this February. Enjoy!

Sincerely,

Denise O'Sullivan
Associate Senior Editor
Harlequin Intrigue

Love at First Sight
B.J. Daniels

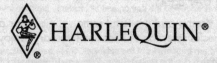

HARLEQUIN®

TORONTO • NEW YORK • LONDON
AMSTERDAM • PARIS • SYDNEY • HAMBURG
STOCKHOLM • ATHENS • TOKYO • MILAN • MADRID
PRAGUE • WARSAW • BUDAPEST • AUCKLAND

This book is dedicated to my mother,
Marcy Jane Johnson, who taught me to cook
and then passed on a legacy of wonderful recipes
that she collected throughout her lifetime.
Bon appétit!

ISBN 0-373-22555-5

LOVE AT FIRST SIGHT

ABOUT THE AUTHOR

Born in Houston, B.J. Daniels is a former Southern girl who grew up on the smell of gulf sea air and Southern cooking. But like her characters, her home is now in Montana, not far from Big Sky, where she snowboards in the winters and boats in the summers with her husband and daughters. She does miss gumbo and Texas barbecue, though! Her first Harlequin Intrigue was nominated for the *Romantic Times Magazine* Reviewer's Choice Award for best first book and best Harlequin Intrigue. She is a member of Romance Writers of America, Heart of Montana and Bozeman Writers group. B.J. loves to hear from readers. Write to her at: P.O. Box 183, Bozeman, MT 59771.

Books by B.J. Daniels

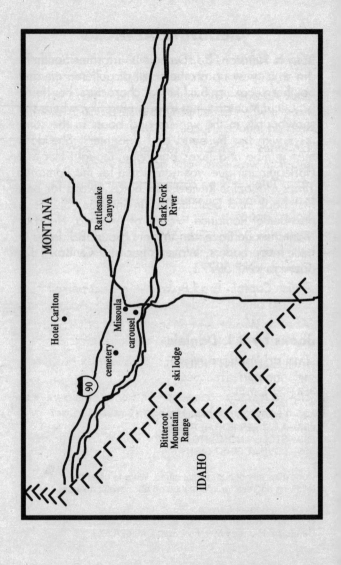

CAST OF CHARACTERS

Karen Sutton — She saw something she shouldn't have. Now she has a cop — *and* a killer — after her.

Jack Adams — The rebel cop was already in trouble when he fell prey to a suspicious woman with an innocent face.

Liz Jones — She had a few too many secrets. The problem was which one got her killed?

Aunt Talley — She's cooking up something for Karen, hoping to tempt her with more than fresh-baked goods.

Detective Denny Kirkpatrick — Jack's friend and fellow cop had once loved the dead woman. Enough to kill her?

Police Captain Brad Baxter — The last person he wanted on this murder case was Jack Adams.

Annette Westbrook — It seemed her passions ran to more than just a good game of bridge.

Dr. Carl Vandermullen — The jealous ex-husband was the perfect suspect.

Howie Iverson — He was just helping his aunt with a little matchmaking. He hadn't meant to get involved in murder.

WHIP UP A BATCH OF AUNT TALLEY'S FAVORITES—AND ENJOY!

Aunt Talley's Fried Pies

1 cup flour
1/2 tsp salt
1/4 cup shortening

3 to 4 tbsp water
3/4 cup drained cooked fruit
(Cooked and sugared to taste)

Sift flour and salt together in bowl. Cut in shortening and add water. Roll, cut in five-inch circles (you can use a saucer).

Place 1 1/2 tablespoons fruit on each. Fold. Press edges closed with fork. Place 2 or 3 pies at a time in 375°F hot oil. Fry 5 to 6 minutes. Drain on paper. Drizzle with icing.

*Canned pie fruit can be used. I prefer using dried apricots, or fresh peeled and sliced apples, cooked with sugar to taste.

For the icing, use powdered sugar with just enough water to make it drizzle-able.

Aunt Talley's Gingersnaps

1 cup shortening
1/2 cup butter
2 cups brown sugar
2 eggs
1/2 cup molasses
4 cups flour

1/2 tsp salt
4 tsp baking soda
2 tsp cinnamon
2 tsp cloves
3 tsp ginger
sugar

Cream shortening, butter and brown sugar. Add eggs. Beat. Add molasses. Beat. Add dry ingredients. Mix.

Chill for at least an hour. Make into one-inch balls. Roll in sugar. Bake at 350°F for 10 minutes. *Don't overbake.* Cookies will be moist and soft and crinkly on top. For crisper cookies, use more butter and bake 12-14 minutes.

Makes four dozen.

Chapter One

Saturday night, March 18

Just when Karen Sutton thought her evening couldn't get any worse, her blind date spilled a full glass of Beaujolais on her best dress. Who was she kidding? Her *only* dress. After five years running her father's business, her wardrobe was more Carhartt than Cartier.

"Oh, I'm so sorry," Howie cried, sounding a little too much like Heloise as he began to explain how to get red wine out of velvet, as well as four other dress fabrics. Something told her he'd done this before. "Here, let me get a waiter—"

She grimaced as Howie called to a man dressed in black, mistaking him for a waiter. The man fortunately pretended not to hear and kept walking.

"Really, it isn't necessary," she repeated to her date and excused herself, less concerned about Howie's clumsiness and the dress than taking advantage of the opportunity to escape—even if only long enough to drown her dress in cold water, if not herself.

"This is your *own* fault," she muttered as she hurried off in search of the rest room. She'd been caught off guard by her sweet grandmotherly neighbor Mrs. Talley Iverson, and while sampling warm chocolate chip cookies fresh from the elderly woman's oven, had somehow agreed to have dinner with a visiting grandnephew.

How could Karen have forgotten how much she hated dating? Probably because it'd been a while. Not that there weren't plenty of men in her life. Builders, bricklayers, carpenters, plumbers, electricians. She even went out for a drink or dinner sometimes with them. At least with those men, she had something in common. And she didn't have to wear a dress.

Howie Iverson, on the other hand, owned a floral shop in eastern Montana and knew the Latin names of all the species. Karen's experience with floral arrangements was limited to other people's weddings and funerals. Did real men still send women flowers? Not the men she knew.

Except for Howie Iverson. She swore an oath never to date any more of Talley Iverson's relatives, no matter how sweet the woman or how scrumptious her cookies.

As Karen turned down what had to be her fifth long hallway, she realized she hadn't been paying attention and was now lost.

Lost in the Hotel Carlton. Great. The wonderfully rustic old resort hotel on the edge of Missoula, Montana, was enormous and half-empty since it was off season. As she tried to backtrack in the maze of hallways, feeling like the little kid in *The Shining,* she heard voices. Hopefully someone knew the way back to the restaurant.

She turned a corner, now obviously in a far wing, and spotted a man wearing a baseball cap knocking at one of the rooms down the hall. She started to call to him, but just then, the door opened and a woman appeared. *Liz?*

The man said something Karen couldn't hear. Liz's hand came up as if to slap him but he caught her wrist and pushed her back into the room. Just before he disappeared, he turned his head in Karen's direction. Their eyes met for only an instant. The hotel room door slammed.

Shaken, Karen turned and rushed back the way she'd come, feeling like a voyeur. Liz hadn't seen her, Karen was sure of that. But the man—he'd looked right at her and seemed surprised.

Was he Liz's secret lover, the one Karen had only heard about that morning? She cringed recalling what she'd just witnessed—and almost collided with a woman coming around the corner.

"Excuse me," Karen said, as the woman, neither acknowledging the collision or the apology, hurried away. Karen looked after her. Wasn't that the newest member of her mother's bridge club?

"There you are!"

Karen jumped, startled as she came face-to-face with her date.

"I was afraid you were lost," Howie said. "Oh, look at your dress! You really should have gotten cold water on that right away. It's going to be difficult to get that spot out now."

She looked down at the huge red stain and was startled to see how much it resembled blood against the pale blue of the velvet. No wonder the man with Liz had looked so surprised.

But it didn't explain the way he'd reacted to Liz. Or her to him. Not that it was any of Karen's business, she reminded herself. Until this morning, she hadn't even seen Liz since high school. Almost sixteen years.

That's why she'd been so surprised when she'd run into her on the street in Missoula and Liz had insisted they talk over a latte at the corner coffee shop. Karen became even more uncomfortable when her former classmate, who had nervously kept watching the door, confessed that she'd done something she probably shouldn't have, then blurted out that she'd been seeing a mystery man, someone she'd met through the personals column in the newspaper.

"I really should get home and soak this dress, don't you think?" Karen said to her neighbor's grandnephew and her very last ever blind date.

She couldn't wait to get out of the dress and end the date, and not in that order. Nor did she want to think about Liz and the man in the hotel hallway. Liz was a grown woman. She knew what she was doing.

But even as Karen said it, she feared Liz had gotten in over her head. She kept remembering the way the two had reacted to each other in the hallway. That was one romance headed south.

Twenty minutes later, Karen was trying to gracefully close her apartment door on Howie Iverson and the entire evening, when she was literally saved by the bell.

The phone rang. "Thank you again, but it isn't necessary," she said politely to Howie's offer to have her dress cleaned. Hurriedly she shut the door, bolted it and ran to answer the phone.

"Hello?" She could hear breathing. "Hello?"

The line clicked.

Karen stared at the receiver.

Had it been Liz? Maybe.

Or a crazed serial killer checking to see if she was home alone? Probably.

Or a wrong number, she thought, trying to corral her imagination and shake off the ominous feeling she'd had since opening the door to find Howie peeking through a bouquet of the strangest-looking flowers she'd ever seen.

But as she started to hang up the phone, she knew it wasn't the date—as awkward as it'd been—that had her so jumpy.

On impulse she hit star 69. The phone number the automated voice repeated didn't sound familiar. A wrong number, just like she'd thought. The line began to ring. *Hang up! You're going to look like a fool!*

"Good evening, Hotel Carlton."

Her pulse pounded at her temples. Had Liz called her? "Yes. Could you please ring Liz Jones's room?"

"One moment, please."

It suddenly struck Karen that Liz wouldn't have registered in her own name. Actually, she probably wouldn't have registered at all. While Karen didn't know much about clandestine affairs, she thought the male lover acquired the room, and probably under some assumed name like Smith.

So why was she still waiting on the line when she knew the clerk would come back any minute to say there was no Liz Jones registered?

The extension began to ring. Liz *had* registered—

and under her own name? Well, it *was* a new decade for women.

Someone picked up after the first ring but said nothing.

Karen swallowed. "Liz?"

No answer. Just soft breathing.

What was she doing? Karen quickly hung up and stood staring at the phone. Who'd answered? More important, who'd called her from the hotel in the first place? She blinked. The answering machine light blinked back at her, bright red.

Quickly she rewound the tape, surprised to find herself trembling. Geez, she felt like a kid who'd been caught playing phone games. *"I saw what you did. I know who you are."* *I'm an idiot. Come and get me.*

Except she hadn't seen anything and knew even less. *Not true.* She'd seen Liz with a man. The lover who'd insisted his identity be kept secret? And now Karen had not only seen him—he'd seen *her!*

She jumped as the answering machine clicked on and Liz's distraught voice filled the room. "Karen? Please pick up. I really need to talk to you. I found out who he is. You know, the man I told you about. I found out *everything.* This is so freaky." Pause. "All right, I guess you're not home. I need to talk to him first, anyway. You know, give the bastard a chance to...explain, huh?" She sounded close to tears and getting more angry by the moment. "I can tell you one thing. I'm not going to let him get away with this. He's going to pay." A knock sounded in the background. "That's him now."

The line disconnected, the silence too loud, too final in the suddenly morguelike room.

Liz *had* called. Karen checked the time on the answering machine: 7:48. That would have been just after Howie spilled her wine all over her dress while explaining greenhouse flower pollination. And just before—

Her pulse roared in her ears. My God, Liz had been on the phone calling her at the same time Karen had rounded the corner in the hotel and seen the man knocking at Liz's door!

Karen felt a shiver. Had that been Liz who'd called a few minutes ago? Then why hadn't she said something? And who'd answered the phone in Liz's room when Karen had called? The secret lover?

This is none of your business. Except that Liz had involved her in it by confessing it all to her. Now Karen felt as if she'd just sat through an unsettling movie, only to have the projector break down before the end. She needed an ending. Preferably a happy one.

"Maybe I should call Liz's hotel room again," she said to the silence, worried that neither of them was going to get a happy ending.

Get a life, Sutton. And get out of this dress!

Chapter Two

It wasn't until very early the next morning that Karen, half-asleep, got the news.

Howie brought it, along with some of his aunt's still-warm homemade fried pies and a spray can of spot remover.

Karen opened the door barefoot, in the old T-shirt she'd slept in and a pair of thrown-on worn jeans. *"Howie?"*

He stuck the fried pies under her nose like smelling salts.

She took a whiff and a pie and stumbled groggily into the kitchen, following the smell emanating from her automatic coffeemaker. What time was it anyway?

Howie trailed after her into the tiny kitchen. "Like I was saying, I have this friend at the Hotel Carlton flower shop. She says the police have been swarming all over the place since she got there this morning."

Sleepily, Karen took a bite of the palm-size lightly frosted still-warm apricot fried pie and chewed, moaning in pleasure. Better than chocolate. Better than sleep. Better than even— She stopped chewing. "What?"

Howie handed her a napkin and pointed to a crumb on her chin. She wiped at it robotically as she watched him pull down a cup and fill it with coffee. He handed it to her.

Police? She took a gulp of the hot strong coffee, desperately needing to get up to speed. Her head cleared a little as the caffeine started to kick in. She took another drink. Her eyes began to focus. They focused on Howie.

He smiled in acknowledgment and refilled her cup. Somehow she hadn't expected to see him again after last night. How long did his aunt say he'd be in town?

"It turns out someone was murdered at the hotel last night," he said as he handed her the full cup. "Can you imagine that?"

She stared at him. Unfortunately, she *could* imagine that. What the caffeine hadn't yet completely accomplished, the word *murder* did. "*Who* was murdered?"

"Her name hasn't been released yet," he continued, his interest appearing to wane as he obviously got to his real purpose for waking her this early on a Sunday morning. "I came by to see if this spot remover works. If you'll get me your dress…"

She barely heard him. A woman had been murdered? Her heart picked up a staccato beat while her pulse buzzed in her ears. Just because a woman had been murdered at the hotel last night, didn't mean it was Liz. After all, it was a huge place. What were the chances the victim was even someone she knew?

"Karen?" Howie waved the can of spot remover in front of her to get her attention. "The dress?"

She pointed absently in the direction of the couch, drained her coffee cup and looked around for her purse.

"You did soak the dress overnight in cold water, didn't you?" he asked.

She hated to tell him.

"I don't see the dress," he called back to her from the other side of the breakfast bar.

She pointed again, this time more in the direction of the corner, as she dumped the contents of her purse on the kitchen counter and sorted through it feverishly for the number Liz had given her. She and Liz had exchanged phone numbers on coffee shop napkins, but at the time she'd figured she'd probably never see Liz again—let alone call her. But her instincts told her that Liz wouldn't have stayed at the hotel last night. Not after learning the truth about her lover.

With relief, she spied a latte-stained corner of napkin, pulled it free and reached for the phone.

"Oh!" she heard Howie exclaim. He must have found her dress where she'd thrown it last night.

The line began to ring. *Pick up, Liz. Come on. Answer your phone.*

When the answering machine came on, she hung up, not wanting to leave a message. What message would she leave, anyway? "Call me if you're not dead? Otherwise—"

Okay. Liz wasn't at home. Still no reason to panic. Maybe she had stayed over at the hotel last night. Karen tried the Carlton number only to get a busy signal.

"Howie, I have someplace I have to go," Karen said, shoving everything but the keys back into her purse and quickly finishing off her fried pie before she looked around for shoes. She spied her Birkenstock sandals poking out from the end of the couch and slid into their familiar worn comfort.

Howie was holding the dress out and tsk-tsking.

"Look, Howie—" That dress had been nothing but bad luck. She'd bought it on impulse because it was on sale and for just a moment, she'd seen herself in the dress having a romantic candlelight dinner with a still faceless Man of Her Dreams. Obviously sale dresses came with dream glitches she should have been warned about. "Here, give me that." She snatched the dress and the spot remover from him, stuffed the spray can in her purse and tucked the cursed dress under her arm. "I have it covered. Trust me. I know just what to do."

"Well, I really think—"

"No time for that now," she said, cutting him short as she ushered him out the door ahead of her.

She left him standing in the courtyard as she hurried to her Honda. As she threw her purse and the dress into the passenger seat, she couldn't help but notice how much the stain still looked like blood. A bad omen.

Omens now, Karen? Bad luck sales dresses. When did you become so superstitious, anyway?

As she drove across Missoula toward the Carlton, she berated herself for being such a fool. She was wasting a perfectly good Sunday morning. The sun shone as bright orange as one of Talley Iverson's apricot fried pies, making the day almost as wonder-

ful, although a little cool considering this was spring
in Montana.

Who was she kidding? It was March and it was
still too cold for the way she was dressed. She flipped
on the heater the moment the engine warmed up and
cruised toward the mountains debating her own stupidity.

Why did she even think the murdered woman
might be Liz?

Well, gosh, could it be the whole secret lover
thing? Or maybe the way Liz had reacted to the man
in the hotel hallway last night? Or the way he'd reacted to her? Not to mention that strange phone call
and the message from Liz?

All circumstantial evidence. Not even evidence at
all. Just one woman's hysterical jump to dire conclu-
sions. She should be concerning herself instead with
how to let Howie down easily—yet firmly. And what
was with him and those warm fried pies this morning? It was as if Talley Iverson were pulling out all
the stops. Karen knew she really should be doing
something about Howie and his matchmaking aunt
rather than worrying about Liz, a woman she hardly
knew.

*You just have to know what happened, don't you?
You're as bad as your mother!*

Oh, that hurt.

Not that it deterred her.

She was going to the hotel. She'd find out who
was murdered. If it wasn't Liz, she'd feel relieved
and foolish. But she was all right with that.

She caught her reflection in the rearview mirror.
She looked like a wild woman, her shoulder-length
brown hair standing out in every which direction!

Glancing around in the car, she found an old navy-blue Scrunchie and battled her hair into semicompliance while she drove. No easy task. Now all she had to do was get control over her life again.

Ahead she could see the Hotel Carlton etched against the clear dark blue of Montana's big sky. As warm as it was in the car, she felt a chill.

JACK ADAMS SAW HER the moment she walked in. Not that she stood out particularly—even the way she was dressed. The lobby was such a zoo because of the murder, he doubted anyone else noticed her. He wasn't sure what had made him look down when he did from the mezzanine where he'd been hiding out. Or what it was about her that held his initial attention.

Her hair looked pulled up into a ponytail of sorts. Stray strands of golden brown curled around her face making her eyes seem large and wide. Brown eyes, he guessed, although he couldn't tell from this distance. Some freckles probably. Late twenties, early thirties. Jogs or works out at the gym three times a week, he figured. Teaches school or day care. Born and raised in Montana. Probably here to meet her mother and grandmother for the hotel's Sunday breakfast brunch. Your typical Girl Next Door. Case closed.

He wished Denny wasn't busy interviewing witnesses. Detective Dennis Kirkpatrick had started the game one night at a bar, betting his talent for observation was keener than Jack's. It had become a duel to the death ever since. But this time, Jack thought he could beat Denny at his own game. This one was almost *too* easy.

BY THE TIME she walked into the hotel, Karen rued her impetuous behavior. This wasn't like her. Not at all. What really brought it home was just how foolishly she was dressed. No coat. No socks. No bra. Now, chilled, she felt nearly naked and knew everyone in the place was probably staring at her chest. She crossed her arms. What *was* she doing here?

"Excuse me," she said as a bellhop cruised by. "Can you tell me who was murdered?" she blurted out, wanting to get it over with as quickly as possible and go home.

The kid stopped, leaned over and said conspiratorially, "I heard her name was Jones. Liz Jones."

Karen felt the blood drain from her face. Her heart jackhammered and the room seemed to spin crazily.

"One of the maids found her this morning," the bellhop continued in a hushed whisper. "Strangled with her own panty hose, I heard. The cops are still here asking questions down in the ballroom but so far I don't think they've found the killer."

Hadn't she known it would be Liz? Oh yeah? And how exactly *had* she known that? First superstitious and now psychic? She didn't like this.

Get a grip. You suspected it was Liz or you wouldn't be here. So, tell someone what little you know and let's get out of here.

She glanced down the hallway toward the door marked Ballroom. All her fears rushed to her head like too much champagne. What did she really have to tell the police? That Liz had been involved with a man in some secret relationship. *And the name of the man?* She didn't know. *What did he look like?* Well, she only saw him for an instant. Did she think she would recognize him again if she saw him? Maybe.

He'd looked surprised when he saw her, probably because her dress had appeared to be covered in blood. It was actually red wine that her blind date had spilled on her. No, he wasn't blind, just nervous.

Karen took a breath. All right, she didn't have much to give the police. For all she knew he could have been Liz's ex, the one she said she'd left because of his jealousy. But if any information Karen had could help find the killer—

BELATEDLY, Jack noticed two things about the young woman that made him glad he *hadn't* made that bet after all.

One was the look on her face as she stopped a bellhop near the entrance. She wasn't asking directions to the dining room. She looked too apprehensive. Too...suspicious.

But that wasn't all. He hadn't noticed before just how quickly she must have dressed. It was a little too cold out for sandals, especially without socks and she wore no coat over her faded T-shirt and worn blue jeans.

But what really convinced him she'd been in a hurry was what he glimpsed beneath that washed-thin T-shirt. Nipples. No bra. She had definitely looked like the prim-and-proper, wouldn't-be-caught-dead-in-public-without-a bra type.

Whatever the bellhop had said to her had left her shaken. Maybe she'd just heard about the murder. Then what had gotten her out of bed so abruptly this morning? It wasn't meeting Mom and Grandma at the buffet. Not that half of Missoula hadn't come up for breakfast this morning after the news of the murder. He really doubted it was the link sausages and powdered scrambled eggs that had brought them.

Curiosity. The same stuff that killed cats. So was that what she was doing here, too? Idle curiosity? No, not as anxious as she appeared nor dressed like that, he told himself. Not this woman.

He looked closer. She was nervously kneading something balled up in her right hand.

Damn, he thought, craning over the mezzanine railing to see her through the crowd. She reminded him a little too much of himself—someone who'd been dragged out of bed too early in the morning. Only he had a good reason. He wondered what hers was. And if they had anything to do with the other?

KAREN FELT SOMETHING in her hand just as she reached the ballroom doorway. She uncurled her fingers, surprised to find the latte-stained napkin with Liz's number on it. She started to put the napkin and number in her purse, but as she took a step into the ballroom, she looked up and saw that the room was empty, the police gone.

No, not entirely empty.

Her feet halted so abruptly she almost toppled forward onto her face. Through the bank of windows facing the parking lot she could see the cop cars pulling away. What had literally stopped her in her tracks was the lone man she saw silhouetted against the window, watching the police leave.

Her heart dropped to her stomach. Could it be? She stared, her eyes widening as she realized he was dressed just as he'd been last night. And there was something about him—

Seemingly unaware of her presence, he pushed open the door and started toward the parking lot.

Karen stumbled back from the doorway, bumping into the wall as she looked around for a policeman. But she saw no one in uniform—and the man was getting away!

JACK WATCHED HER, now definitely intrigued. One minute she was peeking into the ballroom, the next she was reeling back out, looking as if she'd seen a ghost.

What the hell? He moved down the mezzanine to get a look into the ballroom, wondering what she could have seen. Empty. How had he missed Detective Denny Kirkpatrick, the man he'd been waiting to literally grab when the cop came out of his last interview? Because Jack had been watching the Girl Next Door instead of tending to business. And it looked like the cops had left by a rear exit. Just his luck.

He glanced to where he'd last seen the woman standing just moments before and swore under his breath. She was gone! But something lay on the floor. A round white object the size of a golf ball.

He took the stairs two at a time. In the spot where she'd been standing, he reached down to pick up what appeared to be a balled-up white napkin. Great investigative work, Adams. A dirty napkin. He started to discard it when he noticed what looked like writing on it.

He uncrumpled the napkin. A phone number?

Chapter Three

Karen scrambled out the front door of the hotel toward the parking lot at a run. If she could just get the license number on the man's car—

Across the parking lot, she saw him get into a large, dark sedan. From this distance, she couldn't even see the plates, let alone the make or model of the vehicle to give the police. Newer, expensive, American-made, would be her best guess and that, she knew, was worth nothing.

She sprinted to her car, leaped in and started it. All she could do was follow him and hope to get close enough without him getting suspicious.

But as she drove past the hotel, she had the oddest feeling she was being watched. First omens, then bad luck dresses, clairvoyance, now paranoia? What next?

She sped off after the mystery man, the road dropping down the mountainside in tight switchback curves. In the distance she could see Missoula glittering brightly in the sunshine but ahead on the narrow two-lane road, no sign of the car. Had he seen her? Is that why he'd taken off so fast?

She gripped the wheel, heart pounding, expecting to come flying up on his car around the next curve as she careened off the mountain. He probably wasn't even the killer. Just some poor harmless man who resembled the man she'd seen with Liz last night.

Harmless. Karen liked the sound of that, she thought as she swerved around another blind curve. Beat the heck out of the alternative: that she was chasing a killer and he'd be waiting in ambush for her around the next bend.

Unfortunately, she didn't think of the man she'd seen last night in the hotel hallway with Liz as harmless.

She tried to still her hammering heart and quiet the voice of logic yelling *Are you nuts?* in her ears. Come on, she wasn't even sure the man was Liz's secret lover let alone the murderer. He could be the jealous ex or a man Karen hadn't even heard of. After all, before yesterday, it had been sixteen years since she'd even seen Liz.

So why was he driving so fast? And what had he been doing in the hotel ballroom? Had he already talked to the police? Wouldn't that be something if he'd told them everything and here she was chasing down his license number for nothing.

She turned on the radio, needing a little calming country-and-western music right now. A few cheating hearts, a lot of boot scooting and some down-home, baby-done-took-my-truck-and-my-dog heartache. An old Hank Williams tune filled the car. That was more like it.

Unfortunately, even cranked-up country wasn't

going to help. Liz had been murdered and Karen was chasing a man she thought was a killer. At the heart of it, Karen knew she felt as though she'd failed Liz. She should have done something, especially last night after she got that message from Liz on her answering machine.

Sure, Karen Sutton, Ms. Lovelorn, the last person who should be dispensing advice on love and relationships. What did she know about either?

But she had good sense, she argued, feeling the need to defend herself as she wheeled around another corner. There could be something said for a woman with good sense. At least her mother had always said so.

Right. If her mother could see her now! No amount of good sense could explain why she was chasing a possible killer. Nor could any of her rational arguments convince her she wasn't in danger. She'd never been this close to murder before. She didn't like the feeling.

But that's why she had to try to get the man's license number.

So where was he? Maybe she'd lost him. Maybe he'd turned off. Or maybe he'd seen her following him and doubled back to get behind her—

She glanced in her rearview mirror. A car. She caught only a flash of color as it disappeared around a corner but it didn't look large nor new nor dark-colored. But someone was definitely behind her! Was there any way he could have changed vehicles?

Just on the brink of paralyzed fear, she rounded another switchback in the road and spotted the large, dark car still moving ahead of her. She exhaled, an undaunted Karen back at the wheel. Hallelujah.

Ahead the road turned onto the main four-lane highway into Missoula. All she had to do was get close enough to see his license plate. If she waited, he'd be in the increased traffic and she'd lose him.

She floored the gas pedal and felt the car pick up speed. Just a little farther. Just a little faster. She could see the back of the car now, the man's head silhouetted inside, but still she couldn't make out the plates as he sped ahead of her. But she did notice a large dent in the car's left rear fender. Other cars wove in and out of the lanes. If she could just stay with him—

Something behind her caught her eye. Her gaze shot to the rearview mirror, then down at her speedometer—*Oh, no*—then back again at the flashing red-and-blue lights behind her. Her foot automatically came up off the accelerator.

No, not now! Not when I'm this close!

She stubbornly jammed her foot back down as she ignored the flashing lights in her mirror. She saw the dark-colored sedan accelerate and pass a truck several cars ahead of her.

She pulled into the passing lane, eyes focused on the sedan. The sound of a siren screamed over the roar of her car's engine and flashing blue and red ricocheted off her rear window as she searched the traffic ahead for the sedan.

She glanced back to find the cop right behind her. But ahead, the sedan had disappeared in the traffic. She'd lost him. Unlike the cop.

Reluctantly, she let her foot up off the accelerator and began to slow.

JACK WASN'T SURE what he'd expected. Hell, after the way the first morning of his supposed vacation had gone, why did he expect anything to go as planned?

He certainly hadn't expected his Girl Next Door to speed. But he *had* definitely expected her to slow down and pull over when he flashed his lights and siren at her.

And she had. Eventually. Taking her own sweet time. By the time she had, he was ready to call backup to stop her. Backup on the Girl Next Door. What was wrong with this picture?

Then when she'd finally stopped by a strip mall, he could have sworn he caught her glaring at him in her rearview mirror. He wasn't great at lip-reading but he knew whatever she'd mouthed wasn't very ladylike.

All things total, this didn't exactly fit his first impression of her. This woman was starting to cause him concern.

As he pulled in behind her Honda, his lights still flashing, he cut the siren and sat watching her cautiously. Just when he thought nothing she could do would surprise him, she began to beat her fist on the steering wheel.

Then her eyes met his in her rearview mirror again. No mistaking it. The woman was glaring angrily at him. He shook his head. This was not the way to react to being pulled over by a cop. He ought to know.

His radio crackled. "I got that name on the phone number you gave me, Jack. Listed to Liz Jones."

He wondered what his Girl Next Door was doing with the murdered woman's phone number. It kept getting more and more curious by the moment.

"Run me a plate, would you?" He read the numbers off the license on the Honda in front of him and waited.

"Karen Anne Sutton."

He wrote down her address and phone number, then he opened his door and cautiously walked toward her car.

She rolled down her window with the same kind of anger he'd seen in her rearview mirror.

"Goin' a little fast, weren't you?" he asked.

"Do you realize what you've just done?" she demanded.

"Pulled you over for speeding?" Jack stared at her. Her eyes weren't brown. But a combination of blues and greens flecked with gold. Hazel, he supposed, but at the moment, they were more blue. An electric blue that hurled flaming arrows. At least he'd gotten the freckles right. A sprinkling of them ran across the high cheekbones and the bridge of her nose, standing out against her pale skin. The freckles picked up the golden brown of her hair, which had now pretty much escaped from the ponytail. Even disheveled she looked good. Wholesome. Just not quite so innocent as he'd first thought.

"Speeding?" she cried.

"Speeding and failing to slow down and pull over after an officer of the law both flashed his lights and siren for you to do so," he added.

"I wasn't *speeding*," she snapped. "I was chasing a killer. Well, a possible killer."

"I guess I didn't see the distinction," he said carefully. "I thought cops chased possible killers. May I see your driver's license and car registration please?"

She made no move for her purse. "I was trying to get his license plate number. He was driving a larger, newer model, dark-colored sedan with a dented left rear fender. Well? Aren't you going to do *something?*"

He shifted his gaze to the highway. Cars breezed past. Some large, dark-colored newer model American cars. Some dented. If she had been chasing someone, he was gone. And if she hadn't—

Jack looked down at her, afraid to take his eyes off her for long for fear of what she'd do next. "Your driver's license and car registration, please?"

She opened her mouth, then closed it again. Those expressive eyes blinked, still hot with anger. She started to reach for her purse but stopped in midmotion and blinked again, as if seeing him for the first time, *really* seeing him.

It was one of the few times he wished he looked a little more like a cop. Instead he was dressed a lot like her. Faded hockey jersey, worn jeans, Top-Siders. No socks. Definitely should have taken off the baseball cap, though.

Indecision and alarm flashed over her features. She glanced back at his Jeep, the light on top still flashing. She wasn't buying that he was a cop. Why wasn't he surprised? Par for the morning.

As he dug his badge from his jeans pocket, he

noted that all four doors of her car were locked and she'd left her engine running. Worse, she looked ready to run again herself. He just wondered what she was running from. Or chasing.

He held the badge up and watched her study it intently.

"And you are—?" she asked, pointing out his lack of a name tag.

"Detective Jack Adams. Now may I see your license and registration?"

She flashed him a smile about as genuine as Naugahyde. "Of course, *officer*."

He watched her rummage in her purse. She was all nerves and he wouldn't have been surprised if she'd pulled a pistol out of her bag. He wondered if the nerves were her way of showing anger. Or fear? Either could make her dangerous.

With a start, he caught a glimpse of a spray can in her purse. Then her fingers were grasping it and as if in slow motion, he watched her pull it out. He stepped back, now fully expecting the worse. Pepper spray.

That's when he spotted a blue dress in the passenger seat. A dress with what appeared to be a huge bloodstain.

"Drop that and step out of the car," he ordered, automatically reaching for his weapon.

THE ORDER came out of the blue. Karen turned, her gaze rocketing up to his. Only he wasn't looking at her but past her to— Karen groaned. That damned dress! That dress was going to be the death of her.

"Drop the spray and get out of the car," he ordered again. "Now!"

She dropped the can of spot remover Howie had given her. It tumbled to the floor. "All right, all right," she said quickly, trying to calm him before he did something crazy like shoot her. You never knew with these cop types. "It isn't what you think."

"It never is," he said coldly. "Step out of the car slowly and keep your hands where I can see them."

This wasn't happening. Earlier she'd thought he hadn't looked much like a cop. Not with his head of thick unruly sandy-blond hair under his baseball cap and those big brown eyes and that slight crook in his nose in that otherwise boyish face. Not to even mention the way he was dressed.

But he looked like a cop now. And he definitely sounded like one.

Carefully, she opened her door and stepped out very deliberately. Judging from his body language, she'd be wise not to make a wrong move.

"It isn't blood," she said, adding a feeble, terrified chuckle. "It's wine. Red wine. My date spilled it on my dress last night at the restaurant and I should have put cold water on it right away but—" She was babbling, sounding all the more guilty when she wasn't guilty of anything but stupidity. Unfortunately, she suspected a lot of people went to prison for that very crime.

"And I suppose that wasn't a can of pepper spray you were pulling out of your purse, either," he said.

Pepper spray? "No," she groaned, realizing what he'd thought. "It's spot remover."

"Put your hands on top of the car, legs out," he ordered.

Oh, not "Assume the Position!" This would be funny if it wasn't so *not* funny. She did as she was told. She could feel the chilly Montana air under her T-shirt. Why hadn't she taken the time to put a bra on? She tried to concentrate on Talley's fried pies waiting for her at home. Even the thought of Howie waiting for her seemed like good news right now.

The detective moved in behind her. She felt her face flush with embarrassment as she waited expectantly for the feel of his hands. He skimmed his palms down her legs, over her butt, between her legs, then around in front. Of course her nipples were hard as pebbles by then.

All she could think about was her mother. Pamela Sutton, a staunch Republican, City Garden Club member and bridge player, would be horrified—not that her daughter had been arrested for suspicion of who knew what—but the fact that her normally sensible only offspring hadn't been wearing a bra at the time of arrest. And at Karen's age!

Karen closed her eyes as Detective Jack Adams's hands brushed over her. She hated to think that this was the most intimate she'd been with a man in— how long?

"Don't move."

She opened her eyes as the cop sidled around beside her and, keeping his gaze glued to her, reached into the Honda to pull out the dress. That rotten luck, sale dress.

He stared at the stain.

If only she'd let Howie take the dress to the cleaners.

He held it up to his nose and sniffed.

She closed her eyes for a moment, not wanting to even think how the dress might smell after she'd worn it last night and then thrown it behind her couch.

He looked at her over the wad of dress. "Beaujolais?"

She nodded, feeling close to tears. "Blind date."

He reached into the car and came back out with the spot remover. He motioned for her to unassume the position. She straightened and crossed her arms, trying to hide just how ill at ease and chilled she was.

She thought he might apologize. For frisking her. For thinking she had a dress in her car covered with blood—someone else's. For even suspecting she'd pepper spray a man of the law.

He tossed the dress and the spot remover back into the car, seemingly as upset as if the wine had been blood and the spot remover pepper spray. His gaze met hers. His look said he was still a cop. And she was still a speeder.

She waited for him to give her a ticket.

Instead he gave her a smile.

Without her consent, her heart did a little pitter-patter and her knees went soft. She really needed to get out more.

"I've heard that brand of spot remover's pretty good stuff," he said after a moment. "So, want to tell me again why you were speeding?"

She opened her mouth to argue, then thought better of it. He was offering her a chance to bare her soul. She'd already bared nearly everything else for him. And she *did* need to talk to a police officer about Liz. Why not a cop she'd been almost intimate with?

She let out a long sigh and glanced toward the strip mall. "Is there any chance we could talk about this over coffee? Maybe a doughnut?"

Chapter Four

Jack watched her bite into a lemon-filled jelly dough-nut, enthralled. He'd never seen a woman who enjoyed food this much. He couldn't help smiling as she licked lemon from her lips in almost orgasmic delight.

He got her another doughnut.

Between bites, Karen Sutton began to tell him about Liz Jones, washing her statement and the doughnuts down with large amounts of black coffee.

If what she was saying was true, she really had been chasing the man she thought to be Liz Jones's killer. Being a cop had left Jack as skeptical as he was cynical and suspicious. But even he had to admit, he'd overreacted earlier. The woman had knocked him off-kilter, like a load of laundry thrown to one side of the washing machine tub.

He knew he should be more concerned about that, but as he watched her stare deeply into her coffee cup, her hair framing her face, the sunlight streaming in the window, making her freckles glow like gold dust, he realized this woman was definitely a new experience, one he was rather enjoying.

True, her story was unbelievable. Maybe that's why he tended to believe it. Or maybe he just wanted to believe it because of the woman telling it.

"Didn't it seem odd that a classmate you hadn't even seen in sixteen years would be so anxious to tell you her most intimate secrets?" he asked.

Karen shook her head. "I think she just needed someone to confide in, someone she thought she'd never see again."

"But you said you exchanged phone numbers," he pointed out. He still had the once balled-up napkin in the Jeep.

"It was just the polite thing to do at the time," she said between bites of doughnut. "I really never expected to hear from her again."

Jack studied his Girl Next Door. No longer appearing nervous or angry or frightened or suspicious, she seemed only too happy to tell him everything she knew about Liz Jones. She even seemed to forget for the moment that she wasn't wearing a bra. When they'd first sat down, she'd kept pulling the body-hugging fabric away from her skin, never letting either of them forget her recent frisking.

There was something so appealing about her candor, so appealing about her, he found it hard to concentrate. "Did she say how she met this guy?" He handed Karen a napkin and pointed to a spot on her cheek. "Powdered sugar."

She eyed him a little oddly for a moment before taking the napkin and dabbing at her cheek. "That's the weird part. They met through a newspaper ad. She'd put something in the 'I Saw You' column after seeing a man on a street corner."

Jack had seen the personals column in the local newspaper and had always thought only college students placed those kinds of ads.

"Our eyes met on the bus Friday. I wore a blue coat. You wore a smile. Want to get the rest of us together?"

"I spilled my coffee on you Saturday at Hooked on Java. Call me embarrassed. Or just call me."

Liz Jones must have been a woman who liked taking risks. He wondered about the woman sitting across the table from him, then reminded himself that thirty minutes ago she'd been chasing down a man she thought was a killer.

"Let me get this straight," he said carefully. "The man who answered her ad was a total stranger. But Liz started a relationship with him, not even knowing his name or who he was. Don't you find that a little…bizarre?"

Karen looked thoughtful for a moment. "Even when we know each others' names, how well do we really know each other?" she said philosophically.

He stared at her, dumbstruck. Could he have been that wrong about this woman?

She laughed at his shocked expression. "All right, I found the entire thing *really* bizarre. But Liz seemed fine with it. At first. I think something had happened that worried her and that was one reason she needed someone to talk to."

"So, how did you end up at the Hotel Carlton?"

She grimaced. "Blind date."

"I've had a few of those myself," he said with a chuckle. "Only I'm usually the one who spills the wine rather than wears it."

She looked up, her eyes met his. Angry, her eyes had been electric blue. Now though, they reminded him of the waters of a high mountain lake filled with summer reflections. She smiled. Killer smile when she wasn't trying to look innocent. Something hot arced across the table between them. Or maybe it was just the spring sunshine and her smile. She had a kind of sex appeal beyond the cute lightly freckled face, the perky full breasts, the shapely butt, the muscled legs. This was not your typical Girl Next Door. He had a feeling she wasn't your typical anything.

She continued her story right up to the scene in the hotel hallway between the mystery man and Liz Jones.

"What did he look like?" Jack asked, excited that he'd have something to give to Denny. Not that Detective Kirkpatrick deserved anything after the trick he'd played on Jack that morning, getting him out of bed at daybreak.

"Average height, brown hair, medium build," Karen said. "His face was shaded by a baseball cap."

"You just described half the guys in the United States."

"I know," she groaned. "I just saw him for a second. Then later in silhouette."

Jack took another shot at it. "What about the way he was dressed?"

"Blue jeans, jean jacket, baseball cap."

Dressed like that, he'd be Joe Blow Invisible in Montana.

Jack tried not to let his disappointment show. She

seemed so anxious to help. "Anything about him strike you as odd or unusual?"

She thought for a moment, then shook her head. "There must have been *something* or I wouldn't have recognized him again this morning."

Jack wished he could be sure about that. But he couldn't even be sure she'd been chasing the right guy. There were always mug shot books. Or a police artist. But he doubted either would be productive. She couldn't provide enough for a good composite, let alone pick him out strictly from a more than likely outdated mug shot.

"You believe he was her secret lover?" Jack asked. "The one from the personals?"

Karen nodded. "I'd put money on it."

A betting woman. Wouldn't Denny love her? He clamped his jaw down on the thought.

"Why?" he asked, curious, since he suspected she didn't take her bets lightly.

She proceeded to tell him about Liz's message on her answering machine.

"What's eerie about it is that at the same time Liz was calling me to tell me she'd found out who he really was, I was coming down the hallway. She was expecting him. On the tape, I heard a knock at the door and she said, something like, 'That's him now.'

"Add to that the way she greeted him at the hotel, trying to slap him, and his reaction, pushing her into the room as if he didn't want anyone to hear their conversation or to see them together," she concluded.

"You think he's married?"

"Seems likely, huh?"

He finished his coffee. It was time to turn all of this over to his partner. And time for Jack Adams to get on with his so-called vacation. Denny could handle it from here. So why was Jack dragging his feet? Did he even have to ask? He smiled to himself. At thirty-four he knew himself pretty well.

"We need to get you, your information and that message on your answering machine tape to Detective Kirkpatrick at the police department," Jack said finally.

She nodded. "You're not on the case?"

He laughed and looked down at his clothing. "I'm actually on vacation." Kind of.

She smiled. "You must be very dedicated, chasing speeders on your vacation."

He almost told her about seeing her at the Hotel Carlton, about making a bet with himself about her, about thinking there was something interesting *and* suspicious about her, about picking up the coffee-stained napkin she'd dropped, and following her. "Just a chance encounter," he said.

"Just my luck."

He wasn't sure how to take that, but she *was* smiling.

He met her gaze and almost laughed at the tension that sparked between them. Sexual tension? It had been so long he almost didn't recognize it. Almost.

"What now?" she asked, her eyes large and expectant.

Several thoughts leaped to mind. He wondered if she had plans for later tonight. Except later tonight, he'd be frying freshly caught fish over his Coleman

miles from here. *Remember all those plans you had
at the lodge?*

"Oh, there is one other thing," she said toying
with her coffee cup, the nervousness back. "The guy
I saw at the hotel with Liz—" Her gaze came up to
meet his. Fear darkened her eyes. "He saw me, too."

Jack felt his gut clinch. "Did he know you?"

She chewed at her lower lip for a moment. "I
don't think so. He looked…surprised when he saw
me, but it could have been because I had red wine
all over my dress, which as you know looks a lot
like dried blood."

He nodded, remembering only too well. He finished his coffee, then excused himself. In the quiet
of the men's room, he punched in the number on his
cell phone, telling himself he was doing the right
thing. But he wondered if the woman back at the
table would agree. She seemed to have a definite
mind of her own.

"I wouldn't worry," he said, when he returned to
the table. "By now the police could already have
someone in custody."

She looked relieved as she put down her empty
coffee cup. "That is possible, isn't it?"

"I'll try to find out for you."

She gave him her home number and he dug one
of his cards from his wallet and wrote his cell phone
number on the back, still thinking he'd be fishing
before nightfall. "Call me if you need anything."

THE PAST TWENTY-FOUR hours felt like a twilight
zone roller-coaster ride. Karen drove back to her
apartment in a strangely electrified daze, wondering

when the ride would end and the old Karen's quiet life would return. She couldn't believe she'd tried to chase down a killer. Even a possible killer. That just wasn't like her.

No, she wasn't anything like the Karen Sutton she'd been prior to running into Liz yesterday morning. The old Karen Sutton had only read about murder and she'd definitely never been pulled over for speeding and frisked.

She felt her cheeks flush at the memory. Just the thought of Detective Jack Adams warmed more than her face. She'd even thought she felt high-voltage currents at the coffee shop. Crazy. She'd just met the man. He was a cop, for heaven's sake. A cop who'd pulled her over for speeding. So how did she explain her reaction to him? Shoot, she couldn't even explain her reaction to this new fearless her.

Maybe it was adrenaline. Adrenaline and too much sugar and caffeine.

She decided she'd take this new Karen home, get her cleaned up and properly clothed, then wait for Jack's call. Once the sugar, caffeine and adrenaline wore off she'd be her old self again.

When she reached her apartment, she was actually glad to see Howie waiting for her on the front step. She needed a good strong dose of reality right now.

"I have a confession," he said solemnly.

A confession. Great. She'd heard enough confessions for a while. But she and Howie *did* need to talk and she didn't mind the company right now.

She opened her apartment door, just thankful to be home. She still felt numb from the shock of Liz's murder. But at least it was out of her hands now.

She put Detective Adams's card by the phone, cell phone number up. Just in case.

"I'm not sure I'm up to any confessions," she said and turned to find Howie inspecting her poor, deprived houseplants.

"Do you have any organic fertilizer?" he asked.

"Howie, we need to talk."

"Your plants really need water—and fertilizer, Karen."

She decided to take pity on her poor neglected plants, which she only remembered to water when they looked as if they were on their last stems, to ease her own guilt.

"I think there might be some Make-It-Grow that your aunt gave me under the sink," she said, then added, "This isn't going to work, you know."

He looked up from digging under her sink. "What?"

Why did she feel they had never been on the same page? Maybe not even in the same book? "*This.* You and me."

Howie straightened, turning bright red. "You mean you thought—" His Adam's apple bobbed up and down. "But, Karen, you and I don't have anything in common."

Now, *she* was the one confused. "If you realize that, then why did you take me out, bring me pies, offer to water and fertilize my plants?" she demanded.

"I'm sorry if you thought I was interested in you, but, Karen, there's someone else."

"Someone else?" For just an absurd instant, she felt betrayed. No, this weird ride wasn't over yet. She took a wild guess. "Your friend at the Hotel Carlton?"

He nodded and smiled, almost starry-eyed.

Okay. She was starting to get it. That's why he'd taken her to the Carlton. "You took me out to make her jealous." It didn't do much for her ego but hey, if she could help out true love—

Howie shook his head.

She plopped down on the sofa. "Okay, then I don't get it."

"Aunt Talley asked me to take you to dinner because she thinks you would be perfect for J.T. and she wanted my opinion. I was planning to talk to you about it but then I spilled your wine and the time just never seemed right after that."

Her head hurt. It had been a long day and it wasn't even half over. "J.T.?"

"My cousin."

Another of Aunt Talley's grandnephews. She watched Howie mix the fertilizer, wondering how many nephews Aunt Talley had. Well, she wasn't dating them no matter what her Cupid-playing neighbor tried to tempt her with.

The memory of the fried pies almost made her reconsider. What was she thinking? "Howie, I'm not going out with J.T."

"Don't worry," he said as he began to water her pitiful plants. "He's not interested, either."

Karen winced although she didn't know the man and knew his rejection wasn't personal since he didn't know her, either.

"Aunt Talley will be disappointed," Howie was

saying. "She really believes that each of us has a perfect match and that J.T. might be yours."

Karen hoped that was meant to be a compliment. She closed her eyes. Not a good day. "Are there any of your aunt's pies left?" she asked, opening her eyes hopefully.

Howie brought her one on a plate with a glass of milk. He was going to make someone a fine spouse.

"Aren't you going to have one?"

He shook his head. "I've never cared for sweets."

The man was an aberration. Probably ran on the male side of the Iverson family. "So—" she licked icing from her lips "—what is J.T. like, just out of curiosity?"

"He's...interesting," Howie said, returning to the plants.

Interesting? The kiss of death. Worse than "nice personality." Good thing he wasn't "interested" in her.

Karen finished her pie and milk and Howie finished reviving her plants and left. She locked and bolted the door, feeling vulnerable and a little afraid. She wished Jack would call soon.

As she showered and dressed, she kept thinking about the man she'd seen at the hotel with Liz. She jumped when the phone rang, her heart thundering, her fingers trembling as she picked up. "Hello?"

For one heart-stopping moment, she was afraid it might be The Breather again. When she heard Detective Jack Adams's voice, a bubble of pleasure filled her. Pure helium.

He burst that bubble immediately. "I just talked to Detective Kirkpatrick."

"Did they find the killer?" She held her breath.

"Sorry. Denny says he didn't interview anyone who admitted to even knowing Liz."

Karen stumbled into the nearest chair. She hadn't realized how much she'd been hoping the killer had already been caught. "He was in the hotel ballroom this morning. I saw him." He'd returned to the scene of the crime. Why?

She closed her eyes and tried to calm her hammering heart. "I'm the only one who can place him at the hotel last night with Liz, aren't I?" she asked, already knowing the answer.

"It looks that way." Jack seemed to hesitate. "Karen, when you and Liz exchanged phone numbers on napkins at the coffee shop, did you see Liz put hers in her purse?"

"Yes... Oh, God," Karen whispered, seeing where he was headed. "You think she still had my number in her purse when she was killed?"

"I had Denny look through her personal effects. No napkin was found in her purse. Nothing with your number on it. But I checked. Two calls were made from her hotel room last night. Karen, both were to your number. One before her death. The other after."

Karen felt as if all the oxygen had been suddenly sucked out of the room. The Breather. That *had* been him calling from Liz's room. She hugged herself, fighting for air. "He has my phone number."

Chapter Five

"He just has a phone number written on a napkin," Jack continued quickly. Liz must have left it by the phone when she'd called Karen and been interrupted by the killer. "That doesn't mean he knows you're the woman who saw him in the hotel hallway."

"Yet. How long will it take him to get my name and address?" All the man had to do was look in the city directory. Karen's name was listed along with her address. Jack had already checked.

He wanted to reassure her. But he couldn't. Now he just wanted to get Karen out of her apartment as quickly as possible. Make sure she was safe. Let Denny handle it from here on out. If Jack was smart, that's what he'd do. If he wanted to keep his job, that's what he'd do.

"Detective Kirkpatrick wants to talk to you," he told Karen. "It's probably best that you not stay at your apartment. Why don't I pick you up? How long will it take to pack enough for a couple of days?"

"I pack fast when there's a killer after me."

He'd known she wouldn't argue; she was too smart for that. At least, he'd hoped that was the case and was relieved when she said, "I'll be ready in twenty minutes."

He smiled. He also liked a woman who knew when to move quickly. "Good. I'll pick you up."

He hung up feeling relieved. Actually, too relieved. How had he gotten so involved in this? It wasn't his case. Hell, he was on probation, a forced two-week vacation. He should be miles from this case, from this town. Detective Captain Brad Baxter wouldn't like this.

But once Jack was sure she was safe—

He put the cell phone into his pocket and looked up to find his friend and partner staring at him, waiting, and none too patiently.

"You want to tell me what this is all about?" Denny demanded, from across the table at the small greasy spoon on the edge of Missoula where he'd met Jack. "I thought you were on vacation. What's with all the questions about the murder?" Denny asked, more quietly, although at this time of the afternoon, the place was almost empty.

"What do you mean, 'I thought you were on vacation?'" Jack snapped. "You called me this morning with that cryptic bull about 'Jack, I'm in trouble. I've got to talk to you. It's urgent. Come to the Carlton. Hurry.' Remember?"

"It's not important now," he said, glancing at the waitress refilling a ketchup container at a far table.

"Not important?" Jack said, trying to hold his temper as he stared at his friend. Denny Kirkpatrick had been cursed with dark good looks that as far as Jack could tell, got him in trouble with women. It was his affinity for practical jokes that got him in trouble with everyone else.

Denny's call early this morning had sounded like the real thing. Jack had leaped out of bed, grabbed the first thing he found to wear and took off for the Carlton, running scared that Denny truly was in trouble. But when he'd gotten to the hotel and seen all the cop cars, he'd thought it had been one of Denny's tasteless practical jokes.

Either way, he wanted to throttle his friend.

"If this is another of your jokes—"

"I did need to talk to you, but it can wait, that's all," Denny said.

"What happened to *urgent?*" Jack demanded.

"This murder."

Jack decided to let it drop. He had Karen to worry about right now. She was in worse trouble than Denny. Maybe.

"What is the story on this murder?" Jack asked.

Denny shook his head. "Probably just invited the wrong man to her room. You never answered my question. What's your interest in this and why didn't you show at the hotel?"

"Oh, I was there," Jack told him. "The minute I saw the cop cars, I figured you'd set me up just to mess with Captain Baxter. So I waited for you to go to the men's room to give you a swirlie before I officially began my vacation."

Denny smiled and seemed to relax. "Sorry I missed *that.* Couldn't you just see Baxter's face when I came back to the crime scene dripping wet? Imagine what he'd say when I told him that Jack Adams had done it to me."

Unfortunately, Jack could imagine that. He was already on the boss's list as a rebel cop who had stepped out of line one time too often. It was why he was on this...vacation.

"Because of you, I met a woman this morning," Jack said.

His friend laughed. "And you're mad about that?"

"Unfortunately, it turns out she's a witness in *your* murder case."

Denny sat up abruptly. "Why didn't you mention that right away?"

"Because I was hoping to find out why you called me to the Carlton this morning."

He shook his head. "I'm sorry I worried you," he said, actually sounding as though he meant it. "You're a good friend. So, tell me about this woman."

"We're picking her up," Jack said, getting to his feet. He tossed the cost of their coffee and a tip on the table. "I'll fill you in on the way."

When Jack finished telling him about Karen, Denny grinned and shook his head. "She really went after the guy she thought was the killer? She's some gutsy lady. I can't wait to meet her."

Yeah, Jack thought miserably. Karen Sutton was turning out to be Denny's kind of woman.

"Do you have your tape recorder?" Denny asked on the way to Karen's apartment. "I was thinking I'd take her statement some place quiet away from the office."

Jack shot him a look.

Denny grinned, acknowledging that Jack knew him too well. "Baxter's going nuts over this case. I don't really want him to know about this woman you found. Not yet."

Jack wanted to warn his friend about bucking Baxter. Denny should have already learned from Jack's example. But Jack also knew dispensing advice to Denny was like spitting into the wind. "Why would Baxter care so much about this case?"

"Are you kidding?" Denny asked in surprise. "I thought you said your witness knew the murder victim?"

"Liz Jones, right?" Jack had gotten his information from the same bellhop Karen had talked to.

"Liz Jones, *now*," Denny said. "Until the day before yesterday, she was the Mrs. in Dr. and Mrs. Carl Vandermullen."

Jack let out a low whistle. "She was married to *him?*"

"*Was* is the key word here. Nasty divorce. She'd been living in their place in Columbia Falls—he'd returned to Missoula to the house they own here up Rattlesnake Canyon."

"So, what was she doing in Missoula?" Jack asked.

Denny shrugged and looked away. "I guess just finalizing her divorce." Was it Jack's imagination that his friend seemed to avoid his gaze? "Baxter wants us to tread softly. He doesn't want to get on the doctor's bad side by seeing headlines like, 'High-Profile Doctor Suspected in Wife's Murder.' It's hard on a man's political career. And you know Baxter."

Unfortunately, Jack did. Brad Baxter had much higher aspirations than police captain.

As Jack pulled up in front of Karen's apartment,

he saw Denny frowning to himself. Why did Jack have the feeling that there was a lot more to this case than his friend was telling him?

Jack felt a surge of happiness when the door opened and he saw Karen looking freshly scrubbed and smelling wonderful as if she'd just come from the shower. She couldn't have looked more like his Girl Next Door. Except, call him old-fashioned, but his idea of the Girl Next Door didn't include chasing killers.

As Karen looked past him to Denny, Jack saw the flash of interest in her gaze. He'd seen it a million times before. Denny just did that to women and one look was usually all it took for Denny to have a conquest. Annoying as it was, it was something Jack had gotten used to over the years. But it had never made him feel such a pang of jealousy before.

WHEN KAREN HAD PEEKED through the peephole, she'd felt a surge of joy just at the sight of Jack's boyish face.

"That's it?" he asked in surprise when he saw only the one small bag beside the door.

"I travel light," she told him, handing him the tape from her answering machine. That's when she'd noticed the man with Jack.

"Karen Sutton," Jack said by way of introduction as he pocketed the tape. "Detective Dennis Kirkpatrick."

Detective Kirkpatrick had classic good looks and the moment Karen saw him, she knew she'd seen that face before somewhere.

"Everyone just calls me Denny," the dark-haired

man said smoothly, flashing her a snake-oil-salesman of a smile as he held out his hand.

His dark eyes shone with faint amusement—and definite interest as he gazed deep into hers. She'd never liked his type. Too smooth, too charming, too much. But she couldn't be sure about this new Karen. She'd showered and changed and didn't feel half-naked anymore, but she also didn't feel quite herself, either. This new braver, more impetuous Karen scared her.

That's why she wasn't sure what her reaction was going to be as she let Denny envelop her hand in his larger one and was relieved when she felt nothing. Zip. Not even a little flutter. Nothing that is, other than frustration at not being able to place where she'd seen him before. She liked this new Karen better all the time.

"You look familiar," she said, taking her hand back.

Denny grinned, looking pleased, obviously taking it as a compliment as they walked to her car. "Got that kind of face, I guess."

No, actually few men had such a classically handsome face and she was sure he knew it. She shook her head. "No, I know you from somewhere. You look very familiar."

His grin faded a little. He shot a look at Jack.

Jack put her bag in her car and looked over at her, his expression dark as if he suspected it was some kind of pickup line.

Right. She told herself Jack would be singing a different tune when she remembered where she'd seen Denny before. "Don't worry. It will come to me," she assured both detectives. "I'm good with faces. I always remember." Eventually.

JACK DROVE Karen to Denny's favorite bar in her Honda, while Denny took the Jeep and a different route. Jack picked up the tail a couple of blocks from Karen's apartment. With relief, he didn't notice anyone else following them.

Denny led them through the back entrance and down a set of stairs to a small conference room in the basement. Jack took a seat across the table from Karen, wondering what he was still doing here. Denny could definitely handle it from here on out. In fact, the best thing Jack could do, careerwise, was to clear out now.

"Interesting place to interrogate witnesses," Karen noted.

"It's a safe place." Denny set the tape recorder on the table but didn't turn it on. "And right now the fewer people who know about you the better."

She nodded. "I understand the situation I'm in. The killer must be worried about me or he wouldn't have called my number from the murder scene."

Smart woman, Jack thought.

"How did he get your number?" Denny asked.

"I figure he either overheard Liz leaving a message on Karen's answering machine or he found the number on the napkin beside the hotel phone or a combination of the two," Jack said.

"You think he's afraid she told me something?" Karen asked.

Who knows what the man was hiding, Jack thought. "Possibly."

"I would imagine he wants to tie up any loose ends," Denny said. "You're a loose end." He reached over and turned on the tape recorder.

Jack sat listening to Karen retell her story, realizing he wasn't going anywhere until he knew she was safe.

When she'd finished, she asked, "What now?"

"You go somewhere safe while the department tries to find the guy," Denny told her.

"For how long?" she asked anxiously.

Denny shook his head.

"What if you don't find him?" she asked, sitting up a little straighter. "I have work. I have responsibilities."

Denny reached over and turned off the tape recorder. "There might be another way."

Jack had a feeling he wasn't going to like this.

"What?" Karen asked, sounding interested and making Jack all that more leery.

"You say Liz met this guy through a newspaper personals ad," Denny began. "It's a long shot, but what if you were to put—"

"An ad in the personals," she said, jumping on it. "That's a great idea."

"It's a *stupid* idea," Jack interrupted but neither of them seemed to be listening.

"It would have to be something that he'd recognize, maybe might even be looking for," Denny said. "Such as, 'I saw you at the Hotel Carlton Saturday night. You saw me. I know everything. I think we'd better talk, don't you?'"

"Right," Karen agreed. "Bluff."

"Run an ad for a murderer?" Jack demanded,

loud enough he got their attention. Just when he thought the woman might have some sense. "Great idea," he said getting to his feet. "Right up there with chasing the killer in your Honda."

"Excuse me, but if you have a better idea, let's hear it," she snapped back.

"Give the police a chance to find him?" Jack suggested.

"I'm not stopping the police from finding him," she said. "I'm just not going to sit around waiting for the killer to find me first. I have to do *something*."

"She's right, Jack."

"Stay out of this, Denny," Jack warned. It might be Denny's case, but he and Jack both knew he had no business suggesting this to Karen. Cops didn't put their witnesses in danger. Not good cops, anyway. What was Denny thinking?

Jack leaned toward her, his palms on the table. "You can't even be sure that the killer is the mystery man or even the man you saw with Liz."

"Then what would it hurt to run the ad?" she said.

Her logic scared him. "But if you're right and he's the killer, then you're talking about threatening a man who has already killed once. Even a woman with your affinity for danger wouldn't seriously consider something *that* crazy."

"I beg your pardon?"

"Wouldn't it make more sense to hide out for a while and give the trained professionals a chance to find him?"

"Crazy?" she demanded. "Crazy is just sitting around waiting for him to come after me. Crazy is waiting on the off chance that the police *do* find him. No offense, but it isn't like you two are Canadian Mounties. You don't always get your man. I'm sorry, but I can't hide and wait for him to be captured. That's a luxury I can't afford. I have work that has to be done, people who are depending on me.''

''If you're dead,'' Jack said with more force than he'd meant to, ''they'll have to find someone else to depend on.''

She groaned. ''It's not that simple. Anyway, I thought you were on vacation?''

''He's actually on probation,'' Denny interjected.

Thanks a lot, buddy. Jack swore under his breath.

''Then this really doesn't have anything to do with you,'' she said to Jack.

He wanted to assure her he was involved, a lot more involved than she knew or he wanted to admit. But she was right. It wasn't as if he'd be able to help find the killer. Or protect her in any official capacity. Nor did the cops always find the killers and put them behind bars. The worst of it was, there was more than a good chance the killer would come after her. Too good a chance.

''I'm going to put the ad in the paper,'' she said, her gaze challenging his. ''I don't see any other choice. Waiting for him to come after me isn't acceptable.''

Jack shook his head in frustration. ''Let's say the killer is the same man Liz met through a personal ad,'' he said reasonably. ''He sees the ad, he answers it. Then what?''

''Karen meets with him,'' Denny said without hesitation. ''At some place where we can see him from a distance. She won't ever be in danger. There'll be cops crawling all over the place. It will work, Jack. She'll be safe.''

Jack didn't bother to look at Denny. Instead he sought out Karen's gaze, reminding himself that he had no say as to what this woman did, no matter how dangerous it was.

He wasn't sure who he was more angry with. Denny. Or himself. Denny was right. This wasn't his case. Karen Sutton wasn't his concern. Denny was just trying to find a killer. Jack knew Denny would do everything he could to protect Karen. But would it be enough?

He swore under his breath again as he straightened and stepped back. ''The killer isn't going to show. What kind of fool would answer your ad, let alone agree to meet you somewhere?''

''He'll show,'' Denny said with conviction. ''She's the only person who can place him at the murder scene and he knows it.''

''Dammit, Denny, she might not be able to identify him,'' Jack snapped.

''But he doesn't know that, does he?''

''Denny's right,'' Karen spoke up. ''The man will have to call my bluff because he has too much to lose not to.''

KAREN FELT Jack's gaze shift to her again. She'd been aware of him across the table while she was giving her statement to Detective Kirkpatrick. Jack had been deathly quiet as if he had no interest in what was taking place.

She'd wondered what was keeping him here now

that he'd put her and Detective Kirkpatrick together, especially after Denny had mentioned that Jack's two-week "vacation" was actually probation. Wasn't he jeopardizing his job by just being here?

"You think the killer has too much to lose?" Jack asked quietly. "What about you? Are you really willing to risk your life? If he shows, it will just be to kill you."

She looked into his brown eyes, determined not to let him frighten her any more than she already was—which was considerable. But looking into his eyes had a danger all of its own. She felt as if she'd grabbed a frayed toaster cord. The heat of his expression warmed her to the core.

"My life is already at risk, Jack." She certainly didn't need him telling her how dangerous it was to put the ad in the paper. But what other recourse did she have?

Didn't he see that she was only doing what she had to? She couldn't hide indefinitely and she wasn't one to wait for trouble to come to her. At least this new Karen wasn't.

Why did it matter what he thought, anyway? Just because he hadn't written her a speeding ticket, didn't mean he was on her side. Especially now that she knew he was on probation. He couldn't help her, even if he wanted to.

"Let's just hope you see the killer before he sees you," Jack said angrily. He turned to Denny. "It's too dangerous. Too many things can go wrong. I don't like it."

Denny just stared at Jack for a long moment.

"You don't have to like it, Jack," he said quietly. "It's up to her."

"Captain Baxter would disagree with you, Denny."

Karen heard the threat, saw it harden Denny's expression. "Denny's right," she said. "Once I put the ad in the paper, the police can't stop me. They will have to protect me." She looked to Denny for confirmation. He nodded.

Jack swung around to look at her, anger and disappointment in his eyes. Obviously she wasn't the woman he'd thought she was.

But it was her own reaction that bothered her. She felt sick inside with a disappointment of her own. "I appreciate everything you've done to help me, Jack. But please don't jeopardize your job or let me keep you from your vacation any longer."

He nodded, his gaze saying more clearly than words that he was washing his hands of her. "Don't worry, I'm going home to finish packing right now."

IN THE LATE-AFTERNOON light behind the bar, Karen watched Jack pull away in his Jeep, feeling bereft and strangely alone.

Denny's words drew her attention back to him. "I'll put you up someplace safe," he was saying beside her.

She stared at him for a long moment, wondering why he still looked so familiar. "No, thanks. I'll find my own safe place."

He looked as if she'd just turned him down for a date. "Karen—"

"Don't worry," she said cutting him off. "I'll keep in touch. Can I drop you anywhere?"

He held her gaze as if searching for something, then shook his head. "The editor said he could get your ad in tomorrow morning's paper."

She nodded, surer than ever that she knew him from somewhere.

As she climbed into her car, she realized she would have to find a place to stay for a few days at least until she saw whether the newspaper ad worked or not. She tried not to think past that. It *had* to work. She had to draw the killer out and get this over with.

Probably a motel would be her best bet. Something on the edge of town, out of the way. Or she could go to her mother's. The place was like a fortress. But Karen knew there wasn't any way she could keep her little problem from her mother if she did. Mostly, she didn't want to worry her mother. Nor would her mother approve of the seedy mess her daughter found herself in. Pamela Sutton would never understand how a "nice" girl could get involved in something like this.

As Karen turned down Front Street, skirting the Clark Fork River, she suddenly had a flash of Denny Kirkpatrick. Except he looked a whole lot different from the man she'd just met.

She turned around and went back to the city library. The afternoon light was fading fast, the air cooling, making her chilly. Or was it what she knew she'd find at the library?

In the school yearbook section, she pulled down her high school annual. She found a senior picture of Liz not far from her own. She flipped through, looking for a Kirkpatrick. No Kirkpatricks.

She'd been so sure. She felt as if she were losing her mind. How could she have been so positive—

His name hadn't been *Denny* Kirkpatrick—and he hadn't gone to her school. She pulled down yearbooks from the counties around Missoula until she finally found him.

He hadn't been in her grade, but three years ahead of her and Liz in school. She stared down at his senior picture. His hair had been shoulder-length and slicked back, making him less attractive. He'd also had his senior photo taken in his bike leathers, his collar up.

Jonathan Dennis Kirkpatrick had changed a lot in the past sixteen years, but not so much that Karen didn't recognize him. She'd told Jack she was good with faces. Now maybe he'd believe her.

She dialed his cell phone number. If only she could recognize the man again from the hotel hallway as easily.

"Hello?"

"He didn't go by Denny Kirkpatrick sixteen years ago. His full name is Jonathan Dennis Kirkpatrick but everyone called him Johnny K. He was three years ahead of me in school and went to a different high school."

"I'm glad you remembered where you'd seen him before." Jack didn't sound all that impressed.

"I told you I was good with faces."

Silence.

"I know you're busy packing, but there's one other thing I thought you'd like to know. The reason I remembered Detective Kirkpatrick? He dated Liz Jones in high school."

Chapter Six

Jack stood listening to the dial tone, then slowly hung up the phone. Why hadn't Denny mentioned that he knew Liz? No, not just casually knew her but dated her for a while in high school. It wasn't as if something like that would slip your mind. Especially Denny Kirkpatrick's. He had a photographic memory when it came to women.

For several heartbeats, Jack stared at the clothes strewn across his bed and the half-full duffel bag he used for a suitcase. Denny and Liz. Swearing, he stuffed everything into the duffel, grabbed his jacket and his gun, and headed for his Jeep.

He found Denny on the roof outside his penthouse apartment, sitting in a lawn chair, his cigarette glowing in the dusk, the faint smell of smoke drifting on the breeze.

"You didn't tell me you knew Liz," Jack said, wishing it didn't sound so much like an accusation.

Denny didn't seem startled, not even surprised to see him, as if he'd been waiting. "That was a lifetime ago. I wasn't even the same person then."

Jack had to ask. "The married woman you've

been seeing—'' He could feel his friend's dark-eyed gaze harden.

"It wasn't Liz." The words hung on the breeze, both of them knowing he could be lying. He'd lied before. And about a woman. It had almost destroyed their friendship.

At least Denny wasn't the man Karen had seen Liz with at the hotel. At least Karen didn't think so, anyway. Jack supposed that was something. But that man might not have been the killer, either, Jack reminded himself.

The silence between them had taken on a weight and substance. God, what was Denny *not* telling him? Something.

"When was the last time you saw Liz?" Jack asked, sounding like a cop. Hell, he *was* a cop and that was something he couldn't take a vacation from. Not even on Captain Baxter's orders.

Denny dragged on his cigarette and stared out into the darkness. "I saw her last week," he finally answered, sounding as if it had taken pliers to pull it out of him.

Jack swore. Lately, Denny had been acting oddly. More oddly than normal.

"It wasn't like that," Denny said. "Liz and I just had a drink together for old times' sake at The Ox. That was it."

"Whose idea was that?"

Denny stared at the burning end of his cigarette. "Hers."

"She tell you about the man she'd been seeing?"

"It never came up," he said, but Jack could feel

there was more, a whole lot more that Denny wasn't telling him.

A faint light leaked out of the apartment, spilling across the roof into the growing darkness. Jack moved so he could see Denny's face better, so Denny could see his. "I'm going after the killer."

Denny laughed softly. "So it's like that, huh? Just blow off your probation for a woman you just met. She isn't even your type." He frowned. "You know Baxter isn't going to like this. You freelancing. This could get you fired."

Jack didn't give a damn about Captain Baxter. But it could prove to be a problem. He had absolutely no authority to get involved. But dammit, he was involved. Personally involved. Which was the worst.

"I'm not going to let this guy kill Karen, too," he said, the warning clear. If Denny was mixed up in this, not even their friendship could save him.

Anger shone in his friend's eyes. "I didn't kill Liz. Is that what you want to hear?"

"I'd like to hear the truth, all of it, but I don't think I'm going to get it, am I?"

Denny picked up a half-full beer bottle from beside his chair. It was too cold to be sitting out here tonight. Or maybe Jack was the only one chilled. He watched Denny take a long drink.

"It doesn't have anything to do with the murder," Denny said after a moment.

"Why don't you let me be the judge of that?"

Denny dragged on the cigarette and squinted at him through the smoke. "It's a private matter."

"Involving a woman."

He didn't deny it. "I'm going to have to ask you to trust me."

That wasn't good enough, Jack wanted to say. Instead he stared at his friend, thinking of all the times he'd trusted Denny Kirkpatrick with his life. So, why couldn't he trust him now? Because this time a woman was involved, sure as hell, and when it came to women, Denny Kirkpatrick was his own worst enemy.

"You might want to ask to be taken off this case," Jack said.

Denny laughed, sounding like his old self. "That wouldn't make Baxter suspicious," he said facetiously.

"Once he finds out about you and Liz—"

"No reason he should," Denny said, locking his eyes on Jack. "Unless you plan to tell him."

"Why, Denny? Why take the chance? If you really have nothing to hide—"

"Jack, did it ever occur to you that I might just want to see this guy brought to justice for my own reasons?"

He stared at his friend. Could it be possible? Had Denny cared for the dead woman? Jack suddenly recalled one night at the bar, Denny'd had too much to drink and started talking about his first and only love, some high school girl he'd dated who'd broken his heart. "Are you telling me Liz was the girl you were in love with?"

"Like I said, that was a lifetime ago. You sure you don't want a beer?"

Jack shook his head, knowing he wasn't going to get any more out of Denny tonight. "I've got to go."

KAREN'S MOTHER answered the door a little out of breath. Faint classical music spilled out into the night along with the hum of voices and the soft tinkle of laughter.

Bridge night. Karen had completely forgotten.

"Karen?" her mother exclaimed and frowned. "Is something wrong, dear?"

What could possibly be wrong? Karen tried desperately to remember why she'd come. She'd just been driving by and felt a sudden desire to see her mother. More impulsive behavior she didn't want to analyze too closely.

"Nothing's wrong," Karen assured her, but the mere fact that she'd shown up on bridge night proved that something must be wrong with her. And they both knew it.

"Well, step in here out of the cold," her mother said, studying her. "You are taking care of yourself, aren't you? Eating properly?"

Karen nodded. Eating had never been one of her problems. Eating properly maybe. "I'm fine. I forgot it was bridge night, that's all. I just hadn't seen you for a while."

Her mother continued to study her with an intent that was making her nervous. "I worry about you, dear."

Karen realized she hadn't been by in a long time. Guilt, and the emotions she'd kept in check since the murder, brought a flood of tears to her eyes. She glanced away, hoping her mother hadn't seen them.

She desperately wanted to change the subject. "Mom, isn't that Annette Westbrook's coat, that new bridge player I met a while back with you?" she asked, spying the locally made, one-of-a-kind coat on top of a pile on the settee.

Her mother glanced at the coat. "I don't know, dear. Is it important? I could ask her."

"No," Karen said quickly. "I just saw one like it recently, that's all." *In the Hotel Carlton last night, actually. At the same time I might have seen a murderer.* She'd been right. The woman in the hallway near Liz's room *was* Annette Westbrook.

It was time to go. To get out before she blurted out everything and really started to cry. She couldn't do that to her mother. Especially on bridge night. "Mom, get back to your game, please. I'll come by soon and we can visit."

Her mother still looked worried. "I really wish you would find yourself a nice young man."

The answer to any problem. *Except this one, Mom.* But Karen smiled and kissed her mom's cheek, the scent of her perfume taking Karen back to her childhood. That was why she'd come here, she thought, as she turned and left. Looking for that childhood sanctuary where the worst that could happen was a skinned knee or a broken vase.

As she drove away, she realized there was no place to run that she would feel safe. But at least now she knew where to go.

JACK'S CELL PHONE rang just as he climbed into his Jeep. "Yeah?" he said, still mulling over his conversation with Denny, still worried and concerned that his partner had gotten entangled in all this.

"It's Henderson," a female voice said with official quickness.

A wave of apprehension hit him. "You still have her?"

"Affirmative. As per your instructions, I followed her from the doughnut shop and have been with her ever since."

"Good work." He began to breathe a little easier and was glad he'd called former cop Janet Henderson this morning. She'd retired a few years back but he'd helped her when she was having trouble with her teenage son. She'd told him if he ever needed anything to just call. And he had. He didn't want to think about why he'd called in an IOU for Karen Sutton, a woman he barely knew.

"I thought I'd better give you an update," Henderson said. "She went straight to her apartment after the doughnut shop and remained there until you came for her. After her meeting with you and Denny at the bar, she went to the Missoula Public Library. Thirty minutes later, she drove to a house in Rattlesnake Canyon owned by her mother and got out, sans suitcase. Ten minutes later and alone, she headed west out of town."

Toward that strip of new motels, he thought.

"To the Birch Industrial Park. She parked her blue Honda and went into one of the larger metal buildings about forty minutes ago, again sans suitcase. No sign since."

"What is she doing at an industrial park?" he asked.

"Got *me*," Henderson said. "You want me to go in and check it out?"

"No, I'm on my way. Mind staying until I get there?"

"Not at all."

"Thanks, Janet," he said. "I really appreciate this."

"No problem."

On the way to Birch Industrial Park, Jack realized he still had the answering machine tape Karen had given him in his jeans pocket. Already in deep, he called the evidence room and asked that a copy of the Liz Jones case file be expressed to his apartment. Fortunately, the person on duty didn't question the request. Probably didn't realize Jack was supposed to be miles from this case, miles from this town.

Darkness hunkered between the buildings as Jack turned off his headlights and drove slowly into the industrial park. He spotted Henderson's pickup and waved to her. It wasn't until she'd pulled away that he parked and got out of his Jeep, his shoulder holster snug against his ribs, the pistol feeling heavy.

Karen Sutton's blue Honda was parked outside a large nondescript metal building at the back of the industrial park. According to his calculations, she'd been in the building for over an hour now.

He'd expected her to go to one of the motels on the edge of Missoula, certainly not to come to an industrial park. When was he going to learn to expect the unexpected from this woman?

He stared at the building in front of the Honda, asking himself what he was doing here. Chief Baxter wasn't going to like him butting in. Denny already didn't. And Karen Sutton didn't seem to need his help.

But that wasn't stopping him, was it? No, because

the Liz Jones case bothered him. And Karen Sutton bothered him even more. Just not in the same way.

The modest sign over the front door of the metal building read Western Cabinetry. He tried the front door, expecting to find it locked at this hour. It opened and he stepped in, struck instantly by the scent of fresh-cut pine.

No one sat at the small desk just inside the door but he could hear the whine of a saw deeper in the building. He moved toward it, alert. What was a woman like his Girl Next Door doing here? It didn't seem like the time to order cabinets, not even bookshelves, not with a murderer looking for her. But what did he know?

He came around a small partition, the whir of the saw filling the air, and spotted a figure at a long, well-lit workbench, running a circular saw.

With a start, Jack realized it was Karen. Wearing goggles, overalls, a chambray shirt with the sleeves rolled up and a tool belt around her hips.

What had ever made him think this woman worked in day care or taught elementary school?

From her obvious confidence, he saw that she knew what she was doing. She looked as at home in overalls and a tool belt as she would holding a baby, a toddler tugging at her pant leg, and her with that same capable, confident look on her face.

He blinked the image away, wondering where it had come from. Babies? He'd avoided even the thought. The same way he'd avoided marriage.

The whine of the saw died off; part of the board dropped to the concrete, stirring up sawdust. Without the noise of the saw, he could hear the country music coming out of the stereo at the end of her workbench.

She put down the saw and dusted her hands on her overalls. She looked good in overalls. You couldn't say that about a lot women.

"You come to help or just watch?" she asked without turning around.

Startled, he couldn't think of anything to say. How had she known—? He watched her reach over to hit a switch. A red light next to the workbench stopped flashing. The light. Well, that explained how she knew he was here. Or at least, someone was here.

"I had a feeling I'd be seeing you again," she said, still not turning around.

She didn't sound too unhappy about it. He supposed that was something.

"I guess I don't have to ask what you're doing here," he said.

"I told you I have work to do, an order that needs to go out by the end of the month and I'm behind."

He nodded as he moved closer. "Responsibilities. People who depend on you." He had the feeling that was only part of the reason she'd come here tonight. He'd tried to lose himself in physical work too many times not to see that.

"So, what are you working on?" He walked over to a completed pine hutch.

"Finishing up a special order. That's part of it," she said, pointing to the hutch.

He spun around in surprise to look at her. "*You* designed and built this?"

She pushed the goggles back on her head. "You sound surprised."

She could have knocked him over with a feather. He ran a hand over the baby-smooth surface of the hutch, admiring the simple and yet elegant lines. "You do exceptional work and the design is... incredible."

"I'd take that as a compliment if you didn't sound so shocked."

"I'm just surprised," he said, glancing over at her again. "Surprised you're a..."

"Cabinetmaker," she supplied for him.

"Right, a cabinetmaker, not surprised that you're so talented. I do a little woodworking myself, but nothing like this."

"Please," she said laughing, "You're making me blush."

She wasn't blushing but she *was* smiling, her hands on her hips, sawdust on the front of her overalls. He'd never seen a more sexy-looking woman. She stirred something in him, the way he'd often stirred the coals of a campfire. Sparks flew between them. He could see hot embers reflected in her eyes and this time he knew it wasn't just his imagination.

"How did you get into...this?" he asked, sweeping a hand to encompass the shop.

"I was born to it, I guess you could say. My father was a cabinetmaker. I always hung around the shop with him and he let me use his tools. I didn't even realize how much he'd taught me until he had his heart attack and I had to take over the business. That was five years ago. I'd only planned to run the place until it sold, but then one thing led to another and here I am."

He stared at her, unable to find words for what he was feeling.

"I thought you were packing?" she asked, changing the subject abruptly as if she hadn't meant to tell him that much.

Packing? Oh, yeah. He watched her turn back to her work. Picking up a metal square and a pencil, she leaned over to take some measurements on the piece of pine in front of her.

"I got to thinking after your phone call…"

She looked up then, waiting. She wasn't going to make this easy for him.

"…I can't leave yet."

"Oh?"

"I'm worried about you," he said, wondering why the words had been so hard to say. Probably because she didn't seem like the kind of woman who'd want to be worried about. Nor was it any of his business and they both knew it.

"Why are you involving yourself in this?" she asked as if thinking the very same thing. "This isn't your case. You're on vacation."

Well, not exactly, huh. He shrugged and smiled. "Maybe I like the way you eat lemon-jelly doughnuts."

She laughed. The sound had a great ring to it. "Now I know you're not serious."

He'd never been *more* serious. But where was he going with this? What did he hope to accomplish here? The answer seemed to come out of thin air and yet it was as clear and concise as any thought he'd ever had.

He wanted to get to know her better. A whole lot better.

A thought like that should have shocked him. This was happening much too fast. Or at least the thought should have surprised him. But he had a hunch he'd felt this way from the moment he saw her at the hotel—as crazy as that was.

"What are you doing for dinner?"

Her eyes widened. He loved the way they changed color, reflecting her mood. Right now they were as warm and bright as a Caribbean sea in sunlight.

"Are you asking me for a date?"

He thought about it for half a second, then nodded and grinned. "Yeah, I guess I am."

She smiled then, too, a slow, easy smile, that sent a shot of heat through him.

As good as it felt, it made him feel guilty. "I have to be honest with you. I have a little more in mind than dinner."

She raised a brow, shifting her weight to drop a hand to her hip again, but said nothing.

"I'm worried about you," he blurted out. "I don't think you should stay in a motel right now. It's too easy for the killer to find you if he's motivated enough and I think he is. So, the safest place I could think of was with me."

"With you?"

"At my place in the mountains," he continued, surprised that's where he intended to take her. He hadn't taken anyone up there. Not even Denny, his closest friend.

"It's not anything fancy, that's for sure," he found himself saying. "In fact it's pretty primitive but—"

She started to speak, but he interrupted her, determined he wasn't going to take no for an answer if he could help it. "It's only twenty minutes out of town. I'll bring you back in the morning." He stopped and looked expectantly at her, ready for a fight.

It must have showed in his expression because she laughed. "I was only going to say, thanks. To tell you the truth, I wasn't looking forward to a motel tonight."

He smiled in relief. "Then it's settled."

"I guess I can finish this tomorrow," she said. "But tomorrow, I'll find a place on my own to stay."

He let it go, saying nothing. He'd deal with that problem tomorrow. At least for tonight, he knew she'd be safe.

Her gaze held his as she untied her tool belt and dropped it on the workbench.

"I'm not really dressed for a dinner date, though," she said, glancing down at her dusty overalls.

"You *are* for this date," he said, unable to remember a time he was as excited about a dinner date. "The atmosphere and dress are casual, the cook is pretty good even if he says so himself and the view— wait until you see the view. You can see for miles."

That *was* the idea. From the ski lodge, he'd be able to see anyone coming for her. And he didn't mind that he'd have her all to himself.

Chapter Seven

Karen sat back and let the spring night blow by the Jeep windshield. Country-and-western music spilled from the radio to the hum of the tires and the wail of the wind. She sighed with an odd sense of pleasure and excitement.

"If it gets too cold for you, let me know," Jack said as they zipped along the two-lane road leaving Missoula behind.

It had been the new Karen's idea to put the top down. Just the way it had been her idea to take Jack Adams up on his offer of dinner and a night away from Missoula.

After the day she'd had, not even the old Karen seemed to care what her mother would think. She leaned back and closed her eyes. The wind whipped her hair and the cold night took her breath away. She couldn't remember feeling so…free. Or safe.

Safe with a man she'd just met! But she *did* feel safe with Jack and…free as if by leaving Missoula's glittering lights behind, she'd left everything behind, including her problems. At least for one night.

The moon came up from behind the mountains,

washing the landscape in silver. Jack turned onto a narrow gravel road and headed up the mountainside, the road snaking higher and higher.

"I hope you're hungry," he said over the roar of the Jeep. They'd stopped at a grocery store on the way out of town and bought steaks and all the trimmings. Plus Jack had insisted on buying her some doughnuts for breakfast.

"Starved," she mouthed, realizing how true that was as she looked over at him. It was the man beside her who whetted an appetite in her that had nothing to do with food. She felt like a woman who'd just woken from a long sleep to find the world more wonderful than she remembered it.

Not even the large manila envelope Jack picked up at his apartment could bring her down, although she'd seen the red stamped words on the outside just before he'd tossed it in the back seat with his gear. "Confidential. Missoula Police Department Property."

She didn't want to know. Tomorrow. She felt like Scarlett O'Hara. Tomorrow she'd think about it.

And tonight? Oh yes, tonight.

Jack slowed the Jeep as the winding high mountain road ended in front of a small picturesque stone-and-log ski lodge straight out of the 1950s.

In the moonlight, she could see what looked like a ski chalet off to the right and halfway up the mountainside. An old-fashioned chairlift ran from the other side of the lodge up past the chalet to the peak of the mountain.

"Jack, it's...enchanting," she said, realizing it

was a word she doubted she'd ever used before, but that fit perfectly.

"Yeah?" he said, sounding pleased. "But what do you think of the view?" He switched off the headlights and turned in his seat to look back.

She turned then, too, and caught her breath. "Oh." That was all she could say. The mountain dropped in a patchwork quilt of moonlight-bathed rock and pine, to smooth rolling foothills, finally falling away to the distant sparkle of Missoula's city lights. "Oh."

He laughed. "I take it, you like the view?"

"I *love* the view."

He climbed out of the Jeep and she followed him to the edge of the mountainside. She stood next to him, breathing in the cold pine-scented mountain air. That sense of freedom she'd felt earlier was magnified by this place. And this man.

She shifted her gaze to Jack. He stood looking out at the view, his face a portrait of contentment. She felt drawn to him as if this was where she'd been headed all her life. Crazy.

He turned to look at her, his eyes bright with an intensity that raced her heart and made her think maybe it wasn't so crazy after all. She shivered at the thought.

"Cold?" he asked.

She hugged herself. "Maybe a little."

"Let's get you inside, then, and I'll start a fire." On the way past the Jeep, he grabbed the bag of groceries and led her toward the ski lodge.

"Is this yours?" she asked as they climbed the steps.

"It needs a lot of work, but it's all mine."

She shook her head. "I didn't know there were still places like this around." She caught his expression and realized he'd taken it wrong. "It's wonderful, Jack. What a find. It's like it hasn't been touched in over forty years."

"It's exactly like that," he said as he opened the front door. Off in the distance, a gas generator cranked over and rumbled to life. The lights came on inside the lodge and Jack stepped aside to let her enter.

Karen took one step and stopped. "Oh, Jack." It was like a cabin her grandparents owned in the Gallatin Canyon, rustic and very Western, yet homey with old-fashioned furniture, handmade woven rugs, thick slatted pine flooring and a stone fireplace.

"I think 'Oh, Jack' means you like it?" he asked, lifting a brow as he smiled over at her.

"Oh, yes." She moved to a log hutch and ran her hand over the varnished wood. "How did you find this place?"

"It found me," he said taking the groceries to the kitchen. "It belonged to my great-uncle. I hardly knew him but when he passed on last month, he left it to me."

"How wonderful! I mean—"

He laughed. "I know what you mean. The rest of my family thinks it's a white elephant. They all think I should tear down the buildings, sell the land and use the money to buy myself a nice condo in town."

"You wouldn't!" she cried.

He turned to look over his shoulder at her. "I haven't really made up my mind yet. That was something I planned to decide after I'd spent some time up here and really looked the place over. It would take a lot of work—''

"But it will be worth it," she chimed in.

He laughed. "Well, at least now I know a good woodworker."

His gaze warmed her like summer sun. "Can I help you with dinner?"

JACK BUILT A FIRE in the stone fireplace then cooked two thick juicy steaks over the coals, while Karen made a salad to go with everything else he'd bought for their dinner.

"So what were you doing before you came home to run the family business?" he asked after they'd eaten and had fallen into a companionable silence in front of the fire.

"Finishing up a degree in child development," she said. "A friend wanted me to teach at her preschool."

"No kidding."

Something about the way he said it made her look over at him. He was smiling, his brown eyes warm and full of humor. Oh, what just one look from this man did to her.

"I take it you like kids," he said, holding her gaze.

"I love kids. How about you?"

He smiled. "Until just recently, I hadn't thought much about kids of my own. But now that I have, I can't seem to get the idea out of my head."

They laughed and talked in front of the fire until the logs died down to glowing embers. The lights dimmed and Jack excused himself to gas up the generator. Karen wandered out to look at the view again.

Jack found her sitting on the stone wall below the lodge, staring out at the lights in the distance and the darkness, deep in thought.

"A penny for your thoughts?" he said, joining her on the wall.

The rock felt cold and rough but it felt good to have something solid under her. "Thinking about Liz," she answered. "You know, I didn't really know her but I got the feeling that she was lonely. Maybe that's why she let this man into her life so easily, too easily. She needed someone to love and to love her. It's just so tragic."

Jack nodded. "But isn't that what everyone wants, someone to love?"

She turned to look at him. His hair shone like autumn wheat in the moonlight, softening his face and making his eyes golden. "I've always thought people who constantly looked for love were like lemmings rushing to the sea."

"Some people are like that. But I think a lot of us are afraid to even hope there's someone who's right for us out there, let alone that there's a perfect mate for each of us."

She laughed. "You sound like this elderly woman I know. She's convinced there is a perfect match for each of us, like a shoe that's missing its mate. Unfortunately, she feels it's her mission to bring those people together."

He chuckled. "The blind date?"

She nodded. "I'm afraid to think how many more

unattached men she has in her family. She plays dirty, too, using my weaknesses to entrap me.''

''The sign of a true matchmaker.''

''Sounds like you've known a few.''

He laughed. ''I'm afraid so.''

A silence fell between them. Moonlight sparkled in the pines, the breeze whispered softly in the boughs and the scent of pine wafted along in the night.

Karen had never been more aware of a man. She could sense him next to her as if she were monitoring his vital signs. Something crackled between them as explosive as lightning on a hot summer night. Only this was March and she could see her breath, frosty white, on the night air. But she felt anything but cold. Did he feel it, too? If he did, then he'd want to kiss her as much as she wanted to kiss him.

She sat for a moment just looking out at the valley, then hesitantly glanced over at him. She caught her breath. His gaze burned her with the heat of it. She felt herself start to lean toward him as her gaze dropped to his lips in anticipation of their first kiss.

''We should get you inside,'' Jack said abruptly and slid off the wall. ''You need your rest for to-morrow.''

Tomorrow. The word broke the spell. She jerked back, pretending to stretch. ''I suppose so,'' she said glancing at her watch, unable to see the dial even in the moonlight.

She yawned for good measure, then slid off and stood, dusting her backside, trying hard to hide her disappointment. That *had* been desire in his eyes, hadn't it? Or just a reflection? If swamp gas could be mistaken for a flying saucer, who knew what tricks moonlight could play?

Jack showed her to the bedroom, then bid her good-night and climbed the stairs to the loft.

She stripped down and climbed into the big iron bed, listening to his movements overhead. A strong man. A good man. Solid as gold, her father would have said. Just the kind of man—

She shoved the thought away and shuddered to think what her mother would say. "Nice women are attracted to their doctors, not their arresting officers," her mother would say. But as Karen closed her eyes, she radiated in the quiet peace of the isolated ski lodge and the fact that Jack Adams was just upstairs. She felt safe. And tomorrow— No, she wouldn't think about that. Not now.

Instead she'd think about something pleasant. Maybe he hadn't kissed her, she thought as she drifted off to sleep, but he'd *wanted* to.

JACK SAT IN THE CHAIR beside the bed, listening to the lodge settle, wondering if Karen was asleep yet. Why hadn't he kissed her when he'd had the chance? Because he'd brought her up here to keep her safe. Kissing her in the moonlight would have been anything *but* safe.

He smiled as he remembered their evening together and especially her reaction to the ski lodge. He'd liked this old place right from the first, but his family had all argued that the place was jinxed, a true white elephant, and something he shouldn't sink any money into but should get rid of as quickly as possible.

The place had been Crazy Uncle Chuck's dream. Chuck had built the ski hill in the early 1950s, just about the time snow skiing was taking off in Montana. Unfortunately, his dream of a money-making resort never materialized.

The woman Chuck had planned to marry stood him up at the altar. Brokenhearted, Chuck had closed the place before it ever opened. He'd left it just as it was the day he walked out. But while he'd never returned, he'd never been able to part with it, making him appear all that much more crazy.

Fortunately, he'd hired a caretaker to make sure the place was taken care of. But still, it needed a lot of work and so did the road up to it, and as Jack's family had said, what did he plan to do with it?

He didn't know. Except keeping it seemed more of an option now. At least Karen thought so. And after seeing her woodwork, he had a great deal of respect for her opinion when it came to fixing the place up. She seemed to like it as much as he did. He smiled. A woman with exceptional taste.

His smile faded as he reminded himself what Karen was doing here. He'd pushed it from his mind during dinner. But he couldn't afford to do that any longer. He'd promised to take her back to Missoula tomorrow. Back to where the killer would be looking for her.

He picked up the copy of Liz Jones's murder file and reluctantly opened it. A photograph of Liz fluttered to the floor. He leaned down to pick it up, surprised to see that she didn't look anything like the usual women his partner dated. A pretty brunette with brown eyes looked up at him.

He turned up one of the crime scene photos, never comfortable with the death and damage he had to witness in his job. He'd heard that Liz Jones had been strangled with her own panty hose. He hadn't thought to ask Denny about it. But he could see the thin fabric around her neck, drawn tight.

He pulled out the autopsy report. Cause of death: "Blow to the head." He frowned. Why strangle her, then? The killer must not have wanted to take any chances that she might still be alive.

The victim had also been beaten with the base of a hotel lamp found at the scene. No latents had been found. The killer had either worn gloves or wiped down everything he touched before he left.

But while apparently trying to fend off the killer, her watch had been broken, establishing the time of death. Thirty-five minutes after Karen had seen a man enter Liz's hotel room.

The brutality seemed to indicate that this had been a crime of passion. The question was: What passion? If Jack knew that, then he'd know who killed her.

Dr. Carl Vandermullen, the jealous ex-husband?

The secret lover she'd threatened to expose?

Or someone else? Perhaps a former lover she'd dumped back in high school?

Jack shook his head, refusing to believe his friend could do something like this. Sure Denny had a temper and a pretty short fuse, but Liz dumping him in high school didn't seem motive enough for murder.

If the killer was Dr. Carl Vandermullen, then it could have been over the divorce or maybe Vandermullen had just found out about the secret lover.

And if it was the secret lover? Liz had gotten a

room in her own name in a far wing of the Carlton on a floor with no other guests, requesting privacy. She'd been expecting her secret lover when she'd called Karen. A man, the one Karen had seen, arrived while Liz was leaving a message on Karen's answering machine.

Jack thought it pretty safe to assume the man Karen had seen was the secret lover. Because of the time element with only thirty-five minutes between the moment when Karen had seen the man in the hotel hallway and Liz had been killed, the man could be the killer.

Also from the message Liz had left on the answering machine tape, it sounded as if she planned to threaten the man with what she'd learned about him. Add to that, the exchange between Liz and the man in the hotel hallway. Whoever the man was, he was definitely a suspect.

Jack played the tape again, careful to keep the volume down, so Karen wouldn't hear it. Liz's voice disturbed him. She seemed to go from upset to angry and vengeful. Karen was right. Liz's last statement did sound like a threat. Is that what had gotten her killed?

He turned off the tape and closed the file. Liz was dead. And now Karen Sutton had threatened the killer in the newspaper. Jack feared more than ever that the killer would come after her.

He pulled out his cell phone and punched in Denny's home number. "I thought I'd better let you know, I have Karen Sutton with me," he said when Denny answered.

"I figured something like that when I didn't hear

from her,'' Denny said. ''I'm sure you think you're protecting her—''

''I *am* protecting her,'' he interrupted.

Denny swore. ''You're a damned fool sticking your neck out like this, especially for a woman you don't even know.''

''Yeah.'' Except that he felt as though he knew her, had always known her. But since he couldn't even explain it to himself, he sure wasn't going to try to explain it to Denny. ''I also have the answering machine tape. I guess I stuck it in my pocket and forgot about it.''

''Right. Have her and the tape at my apartment by eight in the morning. I hope you know what you're doing.'' Denny hung up.

Chapter Eight

Monday morning

Jack found Karen sitting outside on the same rock wall they'd shared the night before. He could tell something was wrong the moment he saw her face.

"Wanna talk about it?" he asked as he sat down next to her. He could feel the warm morning sun on his back, that indefinable smell of spring in the air and this woman, making him feel weightless as he glanced out at the open expanse of landscape and sky—then at her. Just sitting this close to her was like sitting next to a bug zapper on a hot summer night.

"I keep thinking about the man I saw—" She frowned in obvious frustration. "If I just had a better description."

"Don't worry," he assured her. "We'll find him." This morning he really believed it. Or maybe because of Karen he wanted it so much, it seemed possible. "In the meantime, you can stay here."

"Jack, I've been thinking—"

He didn't like the sound of this.

"—I can't stay." She touched his arm, stopping

him before he could tell her how much he wanted her to stay. Her touch was light and quick, but it made him want to catch her hand and draw her closer. He regretted not kissing her last night. Chivalry be damned, he wouldn't make that mistake again.

"I appreciate you bringing me here more than you can know," she said. "But I feel too…safe with you, Jack."

He laughed softly. "Isn't that a good thing?" Her eyes were the color of forget-me-nots this morning. Bluer and brighter than he'd ever seen them but also more troubled.

"No, feeling safe when you're not isn't a good thing," she said adamantly. "I can't let you do this."

"Do what?"

"Jeopardize your career. You should be enjoying your time off, not baby-sitting me, not making me feel…" She waved a hand through the air.

"Safe?"

She nodded but hesitantly.

He wanted to keep her safe, but if she thought she was completely safe with him, she was wrong. After all, he was a man. And she was a woman. He met her gaze. And if this wasn't sexual tension smoldering between them, then one of them was about to spontaneously combust.

She dragged her gaze away. "After my father's heart attack, I was scared," she said, the words seeming to come hard for her. "My mother and I had always depended on him for everything. I was terrified that I couldn't take over his business and keep it going until he got better, afraid I didn't have what it took."

Jack suspected this woman could do anything she set her mind to, but he said nothing as she continued.

"Then when he died less than six months after I came home, suddenly I had not only the responsibility of the business, but my mother, who was lost without Dad. I learned that I was stronger than I thought. I don't want to lose that strength and the independence I've gained. Especially now."

"God knows I wouldn't want to take away an ounce of your independence," he said smiling. "I just thought you might need someone to lean on."

"No offense, but this doesn't seem like the time to be…leaning. I need both feet firmly under me right now. Sure I'm scared that there could be a killer after me and I appreciate your help. But I don't want to run scared, you know what I mean?"

He nodded. He'd run scared a couple of times in his life.

"I also need to keep my wits about me and, quite frankly, Jack, you're a…a distraction."

A distraction? It wasn't exactly the stuff of *Romeo and Juliet* but he supposed it would do to start. Is that what he wanted? To start something up with this woman?

He thought about it for a full microsecond, remembering that crazy clear thought he'd had last night about her. Even in the light of day it just didn't seem all that crazy. Yet Denny's words rang in his ears like an alarm: "She isn't even your type."

Maybe he'd never realized before just what his type was. "Karen, maybe it's time you let someone take care of you for a change. I'd like to, if you'll let me."

Her eyes shone with tears. "Jack, you barely know me."

He brushed a tear from her cheek. "We can remedy that." He leaned toward her, slowly, afraid she'd bolt if he moved too quickly.

But she didn't bolt. She seemed riveted to the spot as her gaze locked with his until his lips brushed hers and she let out the smallest of sighs.

He drew back, his eyes searching hers. Was he losing his mind? Did he care if he was?

She leaned toward him like a tree surrendering to the force of the wind and pressed her lips to his, sweet and soft, moist and welcoming as she opened, a flower to the sun. He felt something inside him open as well and a rush of feelings poured in, drowning him with a need that did and didn't have to do with sex.

His cell phone rang, jangling them both back to sudden reality.

"It's probably Denny," she said, pulling away. She ran her tongue over her lips, looking a little unsteady.

He knew unsteady as he fumbled for the damned phone. "Yeah?"

"Hope I didn't interrupt anything," Denny snapped, "But we have a situation here. Captain Baxter got wind of our star witness. I had to assure him she was safe. He's fit to be tied."

Jack knew this would happen. Right now, he couldn't care less. But after the effects of Karen's kiss wore off, he just might.

"He's threatening to put me on suspension," Denny said. "If you're smart you'll go on your va-

cation now and let me handle this. So far he doesn't
know you're involved.''

"Sorry, I can't do that.''

"Well, you've been warned," Denny said.

Silence.

"I guess you might as well know," Denny said
after a few moments. "I talked to an editor at the
newspaper. Are you sitting down?''

Jack was, but he still felt as though he was float-
ing. That was some kiss. He wondered what they
could do if they really put their minds to it.

"It's about our star witness's newspaper ad. It
worked.''

Jack felt himself jerked out of the euphoria of the
kiss and drop like a parachuteless fool from high
altitude, the ground coming up fast.

"Maybe worked *too* well. We got two responses.
I guess there's more than one guilty guy out there.''

"Two responses?'' Jack echoed, slamming into
solid ground with a thud. He looked over at Karen,
his heart pounding but for all the wrong reasons now.

Her eyes were wide and still more blue than green
or gold. Magical eyes. But now filled with concern
rather than longing.

"I think you'd better get down here," Denny was
saying. "One of the respondents to the ad wants to
meet with Karen at noon today at a little Mexican
food place called El Topo on Higgins. You ever have
their fish tacos? They're great.''

"No, I haven't," Jack said impatiently.

"You should try them sometime," he said. "Anyway, Baxter says I'm to have her there or else. You,
of course, are persona non grata. But I thought I
could meet you at the newspaper. You bring Karen

and the tape. I'll bring the crime lab boys.'' He hung up.

Jack glanced at Karen again as he clicked off his phone and shoved it back into his pocket. He could see by the look on her face that they weren't going back where they were before the call.

''Two men answered your ad,'' he told her. ''One of them wants a meeting at noon at El Topo.''

She nodded and slid off the rock wall. ''Let's get it over with.''

He almost made the mistake of asking her if she was sure she wanted to go through with this. One look at her answered that question in spades.

He was reminded of the first time he saw her. His Girl Next Door. He could see how he'd originally thought that. She had the look. Except this woman refused to fit his mental mold. What had Denny called her? A gutsy lady. Too gutsy for her own good, Jack thought.

LEAN ON JACK? The thought pulled at her, tempting her, making her ache inside for a lot more than just leaning. But she knew she couldn't trust her body, let alone her emotions, right now. Nor did leaning on Jack in any way seem like a good plan. He confused her, made her feel things she'd gone for twenty-eight years without feeling.

Like his kiss. The kiss had been electric. Her limbs still tingled from it and her knees had gone weak. Karen Sutton. Weak-kneed. How about that? Just what she needed right now.

Oh, why was this happening *now*? Now, when it didn't seem like the time to have her head in the clouds? Now, when maybe there was a killer out there looking for her? Now, when she didn't even feel comfortable in her own skin, with this new Karen acting up?

She had to get tough. That was the ticket. It had worked for her before; she had to trust she could get through this, as well. But that meant finding her own strengths. She'd weakened back at the lodge, touched more than by Jack's concern, but now that the effects of his kiss were finally starting to wear off some—

"May I ask you something? Why *do* you feel the need to protect me?" she asked as they drove down the mountainside toward Missoula.

"It came with my badge," he said and smiled over at her. "And I told you, I like the way you eat lemon-filled doughnuts."

Right, a man who liked to see a woman eat. She hadn't bought that yesterday; she wasn't buying it now. "Does it have something to do with your friend Denny Kirkpatrick and the fact that he knew Liz?"

His smile faded a little.

"He hadn't told you he dated her, had he?"

"No." Jack stared straight ahead at the road.

"Do you think he could be involved in her murder?" she asked and could see him fighting with the question.

"Denny and I have worked together for seven years. I'd trust him with my life."

"What about mine?"

Jack looked over at her. "You really go to the heart of the matter, don't you?"

Always. Unless it involved her own heart. Then she ran. Just as she was trying desperately to do now. Run from this unlikely chemistry she felt between her and Jack. The cop and the cabinetmaker. So unlikely a match. And yet she felt drawn to him with a sudden sense of urgency—

The murder. Of course that was it. The intrigue, the suspense, the danger had ignited a passion she never knew she possessed and heightened Jack's coplike protectiveness.

Once the murder was solved, it would be like Cinderella after the ball. Karen would go back to being the old passionless Karen and Jack would go off to protect some other damsel in distress. Not exactly your happily-ever-after ending, but an ending just the same.

"I'm just being a cop. Suspicious. Cautious."

Jack's words jerked her back to reality.

"Just can't fight that need to save the damsel in distress," she said, hoping he'd deny it.

"Something like that." He drove in silence for a few minutes as if grappling with his own reality. "What was their relationship like in high school, Denny's and Liz's, do you know?"

Karen thought back, glad for the change of subject. "Like I said, I didn't know Liz well. We ran in different circles. I was Miss Goody Two-shoes, Exemplary Student and Nerd Extraordinaire. Liz seemed a little wild back then, adventurous, daring, but that was just from my limited perception."

"It doesn't sound like she changed all that much," Jack pointed out.

"No, I guess not," she agreed. "Denny wasn't exactly a secret lover, that's for sure. But he was a biker, three years older and from the wrong side of the tracks. He drove a motorcycle, wore a black leather jacket and slicked back his hair."

"He told me that he grew up poor and without

much parental supervision,'' Jack said. "I know he got into some trouble with the law.''

She nodded. "I think that was after he and Liz broke up.''

"Do you think he and Liz were serious about each other?''

She thought about that for a moment, then remembered a time she'd seen them together. "I remember this one day when he came to pick her up at school on his bike. The reason I remember it was because of the way he looked at her.'' She sighed. "I wondered at the time what it must be like to have a man look at you like…that.''

"You mean, like he was in love with her?'' Jack asked.

Karen glanced over at him, blinded as a memory blazed bright as a camera flashbulb going off, freezing a moment in time as clear as any snapshot. Jack. And the way he'd looked at her earlier that morning. He'd looked at her the same way Denny had looked at Liz!

She blinked.

Jack eyed her strangely. "Like Denny was in love with Liz?'' he asked again.

"Exactly. But maybe he didn't realize it at the time.''

"I suppose that's possible,'' Jack said, not sounding convinced.

Was it possible?

LOST IN HIS OWN thoughts the rest of the ride into Missoula, Jack hadn't noticed that Karen didn't seem herself until he opened the door of the newspaper office for her.

"Nervous?" he asked, touching her arm.

She almost jumped out of her skin. "No. I'm fine."

She didn't look fine. She looked the way she had the first time he'd seen her. Nervous. Overly anxious. Strangely suspicious. He wondered what had happened to make her that way when she'd seemed fine before they'd left the lodge.

Amend that. Before they'd kissed.

Denny met them the moment they stepped inside the newspaper office and quickly ushered them into a conference room. He closed the door and the blinds without a word.

Jack could feel the anxiety coming off his friend in waves. Were Karen and Denny just beginning to realize how dangerous this was? Jack knew he'd secretly been hoping no one would answer the ad. But at the same time, he wanted this over with and Karen out of danger.

Denny's anxiety today seemed at odds with his nonchalance about using Karen as bait yesterday. Was it just his need to break this case before Jack managed to get them both fired? Or was it something more? Denny's love for Liz Jones? Or his need to hide the truth?

Karen pulled up a chair at the table in front of the two white envelopes waiting for her. As Jack took the chair next to her, Denny shot him a questioning look. Jack ignored it.

"Both replies were put in the drop box outside sometime after 3:00 a.m., after the paper hit the streets," Denny said, taking a chair across from them.

Jack watched Karen pick up the envelopes with obvious reluctance.

"Don't worry," Denny said. "They've been dusted for evidence."

"And?" Jack asked.

Denny looked up at him. "You're still here, huh?"

"Yeah, I'm still here."

He shook his head, but answered the question. "No latents on one. The prints on the other didn't come up in the computer."

"One of the respondents took the time to use gloves?" Jack asked in disbelief.

"Looks that way," Denny said.

Karen opened the first envelope, read the contents, then handed the letter to Jack.

He read the words scrawled in blue ink: "Meet me at the El Topo at noon today."

The second letter was even more to the point and neatly typed. "Tomorrow evening. Five-fifteen p.m. Ride the carousel. Come alone."

"I've already got things ready for your noon meeting," Denny was saying. "I think what we'll do is—"

"Why would he want to meet in broad daylight?" Jack asked.

Denny looked up, irritated. "Who knows? Who cares? Maybe because he's the secret lover but not the killer and he's ready to come out of hiding."

"Then why not just go to the police?" Jack persisted. "And why noon today? Why the rush?"

"I guess he's anxious to get this over with," Denny said, getting more angry at Jack's butting in.

"That's exactly what I'm afraid of," Jack noted. "That he wants to get it over with. But you have to

ask yourself, why would he take the chance of showing up today in broad daylight?''

"Because he thinks she already knows him,"
Denny said impatiently. "He needs to find out just
what she *does* know, who she's told and what she
wants for her silence."

"Blackmail." Jack shook his head. "I don't like
anything about this."

"I think you've already made that abundantly
clear," Denny said. "But like I told you. Karen will
be protected. We're going to wire her for sound.
We'll be able to hear her as well as talk to her all
the time it's going down. She will stay a safe distance away, under wraps. All she has to do is say,
'It's him,' and we move in. Simple."

These kinds of things were never that simple.
"What if he hangs back looking for her, hoping for
an opening with a high-caliber rifle?"

"Look, Jack, I hate to pull rank on you, but you're
interfering in my investigation. I'm asking you to
stay out of it. If you don't—"

"I want him there," Karen said.

They both turned to look at her. Jack had almost
forgotten she was there. He suspected Denny had, as
well. But Jack hadn't forgotten that she hadn't
wanted to lean on him. What had changed?

"I want Jack at the meeting," she repeated. "If
it's what he wants."

Jack smiled. "Nothing would have kept me away
anyway."

Denny raked a hand through his dark hair. "He's
off duty, the same as a civilian, Karen. He has no
business or authority—"

"If he's not there, I won't be, either," she said, getting to her feet.

Denny's jaw tensed. He studied her for a moment, then gave her one of his killer smiles. "This is your show, sweetheart."

FROM HER BIRD'S EYE VIEW, Karen glanced at the small Mexican food restaurant across the street and tried to still the butterflies as big as vultures circling in her stomach.

"How are you doing?" Jack asked softly into her earpiece.

Jack had left to take his position somewhere down on the street soon after she'd been wired. He'd said he wanted to check out the equipment. Karen knew he had to keep his distance because of his probation. But she also suspected it was more than that. He would want to position himself where he could stop this stakeout if he felt he needed to.

Denny stood nearby looking out the same window, at the same café, waiting, just like her.

"Fine," she said.

"It's not too late to back out," Jack said quietly.

Denny looked over at her and shook his head. "Guy just doesn't quit, does he?"

"I'm fine," she repeated. "Let's just hope this is the one." She tried to still the trembling in her hands as she studied the diners at the café through the high-powered binoculars. She wasn't looking forward to doing this again tonight if this wasn't the right man.

The café was small, with just a few tables inside and a half-dozen patio tables with umbrellas outside. Right now, most of the tables were filled.

Denny glanced at his watch. "Twelve noon. Do you see anyone who looks even vaguely familiar?"

She shook her head. She'd been watching the café since a quarter after eleven but she hadn't seen anyone who looked familiar. The place was busy, but no man came in alone, waiting for her.

"I'm going down there," Denny said. "Let us know if you see anyone who could be the guy."

She nodded and continued to scan the tables through the binoculars. Another five minutes passed. "Maybe he's not going to show," she said, then realized a half-dozen cops were listening to her.

Every woman's dream to have that many men hanging on her every word. The lame thought made her realize how scared she was. How nuts this was making her. Maybe Jack was right. Maybe putting an ad in the paper had been a fool idea. What killer in his right mind would—

She suddenly noticed a table at the back, inside the building. Moments before the table had emptied out. But now she could see a man sitting alone with his back to her.

"I see someone," she said.

"Is it him?" Denny asked. "Where is he sitting?"

She focused the binoculars on the lone man. But between the sun's glare off the windows and one of the umbrellas on a table outside flapping in the breeze, her view was obstructed.

"I can't tell from here," she answered, still straining to get a clear view of him. "He's in the far back."

Karen waited to see if anyone joined him. He did appear to be expecting someone. Her?

She hesitated a moment longer. "I'm going down to get a closer look."

"Negative," Jack snapped. "Stay there. Wait for him to move."

Karen watched the man a few moments longer through the binoculars. She knew going anywhere near the café would be dangerous if the man was the killer. But the way he had just suddenly appeared, she suspected he'd come in through some back way. Through the kitchen? She feared he'd leave the same way and she wouldn't get a look at him.

"Stay put, Karen," Jack ordered. "Denny, can you see from where you are? Denny? Are you picking up?"

Denny still hadn't answered by the time Karen reached the street.

"Dammit, Karen," she heard Jack say into her earpiece as she must have come into his view.

"I'm just going to take a quick look," she said quietly and started across the one-way side street.

"DENNY?" Jack radioed again. Silence. Where the hell was he? Jack watched Karen advance toward the café, the hair on his neck prickling with foreboding. Dammit, he didn't like this.

He told himself he knew Denny. His partner must have moved in too close to use his radio. That had to be it.

He held his breath as Karen disappeared behind one of the umbrellas on a patio table, then disappeared altogether as she rounded the corner of the building and dropped out of his sight.

"Karen?" No answer.

His earlier foreboding turned to dread and a terrible feeling of impending doom. "Denny? Have you got her?"

Silence.

His cop training argued that if he moved now, he'd blow the stakeout, ruin any chance Karen might have of identifying the man, and more than likely spook the suspect and allow him to escape.

But right now Jack didn't feel like a cop and it had nothing to do with being on probation or a forced two-week vacation. He swore and started to move in, telling himself he didn't give a damn about anything but getting Karen out of there.

"Jack, I'm almost there."

Her voice stopped him. That and the clatter of dishes. She must have gone around back and in through the kitchen. "You've got five seconds and I'm coming after you," he said to her. Five. Four. Three. Two.

"It's not him," Karen whispered, sounding disappointed. "He's not the man I saw with Liz."

Jack felt the tension rush out of him. He closed his eyes. "Get out of there," he told her. But his relief was short-lived. Now they'd have to do this again tonight.

"It's a wrap, then," Denny said over the radio, sounding more disappointed than Jack. Just as Jack had suspected, Denny had gotten too close to use his radio and had turned it off. Denny always had to be where the action was.

"Wait a minute," Jack heard Karen say. "He's not the man I saw with Liz, but, Jack, I saw him at the hotel Saturday night."

Jack froze. The man in the back of the café got to his feet and started to leave by the side door.

"It's Vandermullen," Denny barked over the radio. "Move in."

"Karen, get out of there," Jack ordered as the other detectives swarmed the café.

Dr. Carl Vandermullen? Liz's ex-husband had answered the ad? God, could Captain Baxter have been wrong about Carl Vandermullen?

Jack took the stairs from his hiding place and came out of the building just as Karen emerged from the café.

She saw him and stopped at the curb on the side street. He started across the street, feeling her gaze, feeling a connection that he could no more explain than he could levitate. Just seeing her filled him with such a rush of emotions that he felt himself smiling like a fool at her.

She smiled back.

Out of the corner of his eye, Jack saw the car.

"Look out!" he cried, but his words were drowned out by the roar of the engine and the squeal of tires as the car turned the corner and bored down on Karen.

Chapter Nine

Jack dove for her. The car roared past, so close he could feel the heat of the engine and the rush of displaced air.

He and Karen hit the sidewalk and rolled into one of the patio tables, coming to a dish-crashing stop.

He looked down at the woman in his arms. Her eyes were closed, her face pale. "Karen?" he cried, fear making his voice crack.

She opened her eyes, then seemed to focus on his face, and smiled. "You really take this protection stuff seriously, don't you."

He laughed and shook his head, amazed she was all right, amazed how relieved he was. In those few seconds before she'd opened her eyes, his life stopped.

"You're sure you're all right?" he asked, relief making him downright giddy as he helped her to her feet.

"I'm fine." Her smile seemed to attest to that fact. "Nothing appears to be broken."

What's a few scrapes and scratches to this woman, he thought smiling back at her. He felt as though he'd been breathing laughing gas. He could hear voices of people around them, a faint distant roar of questions and exclamations. "Are they all right? What happened?"

"Did you see that?"

"A car tried to run them down. Did anyone get the license plate number?"

Jack felt as if they were the only two people in the world. He watched her brush at the dirt on her shirt and jeans. "It's a good thing you're tough."

"Is that what I am?" she asked, looking up at him. "What happened to stubborn, foolhardy and reckless?"

"You're still all those and a whole lot more," he said, realizing just how true that was.

"Jack, that car purposely tried to run me down," she said and he noticed that her hand trembled as she brushed hair back from her eyes. He saw that she finally knew just how much danger she was in.

He felt himself shaking, as well. From the close call. From relief. And anger. He would get the person who'd tried to kill Karen. If it was the last thing he did.

"Don't worry," Jack said, slipping his arm around her shoulders and pulling her to him. She filled in the hollow at his side, fitting against him as if made for him. "I'll find the person who did this."

Denny rushed up and the rest of the world returned in a commotion of sounds and sights. A flurry of uniforms forced back the crowd that had gathered as Denny hustled Jack and Karen out of the way and out of earshot from everyone else.

"Did you get a make on the car?" Denny asked quickly. "A plate?"

Jack shook his head. He'd only seen the car out of the corner of his eye. The rest of the time, his gaze had been locked on Karen.

Denny looked to Karen.

She drew away from Jack's embrace, standing tall, standing on her own two feet. He watched her gain her composure again. "It was a large, brown American-made car with tinted windows."

"What about the driver?" Denny asked. "Could it have been the same man you just saw at the El Topo?"

"I didn't get a look at the driver," Karen said.

"Me, either," Jack admitted.

Denny looked discouraged but asked Karen, "You said you saw the man in the restaurant at the Carlton the night of the murder?"

She nodded. "He was dressed in all black. My date mistook him for a waiter and tried to call him over to our table when wine got spilled on my dress."

Jack exchanged a look with Denny. He had a feeling they were thinking the same thing.

"You're sure?" Denny asked.

She nodded. "Who is he?"

"Well, up until last Friday, he was Liz Jones's husband, Dr. Carl Vandermullen," Denny told her. "Liz's divorce was final just twenty-four hours before her death."

Karen let out a gasp. "The jealous ex Liz talked about?"

Jack shrugged, although he suspected Dr. Vandermullen was the man Liz had referred to. The question was, what was he doing at the El Topo? Had he been the one who'd answered Karen's ad? It certainly appeared so. But why?

Dr. Vandermullen had motive and opportunity and he certainly looked guilty right now, the way he'd disappeared so quickly from the El Topo. Captain Baxter wasn't going to like it, but Dr. Vandermullen was now a suspect.

A uniformed officer motioned to Denny and he nodded and shifted his gaze back to Jack. Jack could see that something was wrong and wasn't surprised when Denny said, "Captain Baxter wants to see you and me. Now." Jack waited for the other shoe to drop. He could tell by Denny's expression there was more and he knew it had to do with Karen.

"Baxter's given orders for Karen to be taken into protective custody," Denny said.

"Can he do that?" Karen cried, looking even more shaken.

"No, he can't," Jack assured her.

"He can if he feels she's a danger to herself," Denny said evenly. "He's holding her pending a psychiatric evaluation. He thinks by putting an ad in the newspaper advertising for the murderer, she has a death wish and might be suicidal."

"That's crap, and you know it," Jack argued.

"You can tell Baxter that when you see him," Denny said.

Karen glanced over at Jack, a silent pleading in her gaze as two uniformed officers appeared to escort her away.

"Don't worry," Jack whispered, his gaze holding hers until the connection was broken by the officers.

He noticed two other uniforms standing by and knew they'd been sent for him. Denny said nothing as he headed for the waiting police car. Jack followed, the uniformed cops right behind him.

JACK AND DENNY found Captain Brad Baxter pacing in front of his office window. He was an athletic-looking man in his early fifties with only slightly graying brown hair. He looked more like a former tennis coach than a police captain.

He motioned for them to close the door and sit down, his movements agitated and obviously angry.

"What the hell is going on?" he demanded the moment they'd taken the chairs opposite his desk, the question shouted at Denny. "I find out you have a witness then hear that you almost got her killed in some unauthorized surveillance?"

Jack said nothing, knowing Baxter would get to him in due time.

Denny quickly filled Baxter in on what had happened.

The captain walked to the window, his back to them. "You saw the car that almost ran down your witness? Was it Vandermullen's?"

"As far as we know, he was on foot. The car was a large, dark, American-made sedan with tinted windows. That's all we have."

"So you can't be sure Vandermullen has anything to do with the murder, right?" Baxter asked turning around to glare at them. "Did anyone get a license plate?"

"The plates were covered with dirt," Denny said.

Baxter swore. "What about Vandermullen?"

"I have an APB out on him."

"What?" Baxter barked.

"At this point he's only wanted for questioning. Our witness can place him at the Hotel Carlton the night of the murder."

Baxter didn't look happy to hear that. "You take this slowly, carefully," he warned Denny. "Dr. Vandermullen is a powerful man in this town."

Denny had been right. Baxter was acting more paranoid than usual about the case. Was it just because the victim had been Dr. Vandermullen's wife?

"What about this woman?" Baxter asked, this time looking at Jack. "Is she a reliable witness?"

Jack nodded.

"She saw Vandermullen at the hotel Saturday night, but says he wasn't the man she saw *with* the murder victim," Denny said.

"Can she ID the man she saw with Liz Jones?" Baxter asked.

"Yes." Denny shot a look at Jack, daring him to disagree. "That's why she put the ad in the paper. She's determined to find him before he finds her. He also saw *her* that night and it appears he called her from the hotel following the murder."

The captain had the look of a man who'd missed a good party he should have been invited to. "It seems you've been doing a lot of investigating on your own. Why is that?"

Denny glanced over at Jack. "Everything happened so fast. When I got on a lead I just followed it."

Baxter nodded, obviously not liking it.

"We have another meeting set up this evening at the carousel with the second respondent from her ad," Denny added hurriedly.

Baxter shook his head. "I don't want her life at risk again, Kirkpatrick."

"No, sir," he said quickly. "She's in protective custody with the men you sent for her. But even if she is released from the safe house after her psychiatric evaluation, we're planning to use a decoy at this second meeting, take photographs of the suspect that we can later show Ms. Sutton and keep a tail on the suspect."

"No more foul-ups," Baxter ordered. "You make sure nothing happens to that woman. I want her guarded at all times and I want to know when Dr. Vandermullen is picked up. And Kirkpatrick, I don't want you sneezing without me knowing about it."

Denny nodded and got up to leave, Jack right behind him.

"Not you, Adams," Baxter snapped. "And Kirkpatrick? Wait outside my office. I'm not through with you yet."

JACK SAT BACK DOWN across from Captain Baxter's desk as the door closed after Denny.

"What the hell are you doing getting involved in this investigation?" he demanded. "I ought to fire you and have you thrown in jail."

Baxter could do it, too, Jack thought. "Captain, take me off probation, put me on the case. Let me come back and work it."

"Do I need to remind you that you are on probation because I don't like your attitude, Adams? Do you really think I would put you on the case after you have compromised the investigation? Not on your life. As of this moment, you're suspended. I want your badge and your gun.''

Jack shouldn't have been surprised. Baxter had been bucking for this from the first day he'd taken over the department. Jack knew he rubbed Baxter the wrong way. But Jack never thought it would come to this. Without a word, Jack handed over his badge and laid his pistol on the captain's desk.

"If you don't stay out of this, I *will* fire you and have you thrown in jail," Baxter threatened. "I don't want to see your face again for two weeks. Now get out of here.''

Jack left. He'd have to be more careful so Baxter didn't see him, but he definitely wasn't going anywhere. He was going to find out who'd tried to kill Karen. But first he had to find out where Baxter had her hidden.

He passed Denny who gave him an I-told-you-so look before going back into Baxter's office. Jack waited for his friend outside the building.

"I can't help you," Denny said irritably, before Jack could even tell him what he wanted. He kept walking. "Baxter's pulled me off the case.''

"What?'' Jack stumbled and had to hurry to catch up with his partner. Baxter had sounded as though he was going to let Denny stay on the case. What had changed his mind? Jack had a feeling it was his fault. "I'm sorry.''

"It's not your fault.'' Denny glanced over at him and slowed his pace a little. "You still have a job?''

"For the moment," Jack said. "I need to know where Baxter's had Karen taken."

Denny shook his head.

"I'm worried about her, Denny. Baxter is too busy trying to be politically correct and not upset Vandermullen and his strong political ties. I'm afraid someone's going to mess up and Karen's going to pay for it."

His partner slowed to a stop. He looked back to be sure they hadn't been followed. "Come on." He took Jack to an out-of-the-way bar up by the old railroad depot.

Al and Vic's was a narrow, dark bar with a zigzag of dark and light tile on the floor and a couple of pool tables in the back. Denny led him to an end stool away from the other customers, who all seemed to be older regulars.

"You've always bucked authority, but this case isn't the one to cross Baxter on," Denny said quietly. "He's afraid of the bad publicity, not to mention the grief a man like Dr. Vandermullen could heap on him. Baxter'll have your badge if you don't leave this alone."

Jack knew what his partner was saying was true. "I'll have to take my chances."

Denny stared at him wide-eyed for a moment then laughed and ordered them both drafts. "What has this woman done to you?"

Jack wished he knew. He waited until the bartender slid the beers in front of them before he tried to explain it to Denny—and himself. "The first time I saw her, something struck me about her." He laughed. "Struck me like a bolt of lightning."

Denny chuckled. "What? Love at first sight? You have to be kidding."

"More like *cursed* at first sight," he said shaking his head. "I swear, Denny, from the moment I laid eyes on that woman, everything…changed. I don't know which end is up."

Denny only stared at him.

"I know you think I'm crazy."

Still his friend said nothing.

"The question is, are you going to help me?" Jack asked.

Denny sipped his beer. "You'll get us both fired, you know that?" He took another drink. "I'll see what I can find out."

"Thanks, buddy. I owe you."

"Yeah, and I think this is the way you're repaying me for all those practical jokes." He got up to leave but then hesitated. "You'd better figure out what the deal is with you and this woman and soon. A cop can't afford to be walking around not knowing which end is up, you know. Not even one on suspension."

Jack nodded.

"Give me an hour. Where can I reach you?"

"Right here," Jack said.

IN A ROOM on the top floor of a small brick hotel overlooking the Clark Fork River and the city carousel, Karen thumbed through the last book of mug shots she'd been given. After a while all the photos of the men had started to look alike. She glanced at her guards, two uniformed officers playing cards, the reality of her situation never more clear—or painful.

She felt truly afraid for the first time and alone

even with the officers there. The full impact of what had happened earlier had finally hit her. Someone had tried to run her down in the street. Tried to kill her.

And now Captain Brad Baxter had ordered her into protective custody, pending a psychiatric evaluation. She doubted he really thought her ad in the newspaper was a death wish. Maybe he was just trying to protect her.

But she thought it was more his way of warning Jack and Denny. This was his murder case and no one had better get in his way—including the star witness.

She couldn't believe that just because for one instant she happened to see a man in a hallway, her life was now in danger and her freedom taken from her. At least temporarily. She hoped.

"Don't worry," Jack had said. But he'd looked worried. And so had Denny.

So where did that leave her? In the hands of men she didn't know. Men she didn't necessarily trust. She liked that even less than she'd liked being dependent on Jack. Thank God he'd been there today. She just hoped she hadn't gotten him fired. Or jailed.

She slammed the mug book closed and went to stand at the window to stare out at the dying afternoon. She saw the line of people buying tokens for the carousel across the river and wondered where Jack was. By now, he could be miles from here. She wished she could talk to him, but she knew any more contact might only lose him his job. She'd been afraid of leaning on him too much and now she ached to hear his voice.

Just the memory of being in his arms—

What was she doing standing here daydreaming about Jack? There was a killer out there who wanted her dead.

As she stood at the window, the day fading fast, she began to formulate a plan to escape. She couldn't accomplish anything locked up here. Who knew how long the psychiatric evaluation would take? And who knew what the outcome would be? Maybe she was nuts for putting the ad in the paper.

The next meeting was in less than an hour with the man who'd written the second letter. This time it could be Liz's secret lover but Karen was too far from the carousel to recognize him. She'd seen him twice now. What was it about him the second time that made her so sure it had been him? She didn't know.

She wanted him caught. The only way that was going to happen was for her to be there. Identify him. So she could get her life back.

Funny, but her old life didn't have as much appeal, she thought remembering the ski lodge and Jack and that overwhelming feeling of belonging there. Pure fantasy. She'd felt safe there and she was sure that was the big appeal.

Why was she trying so hard to rationalize her feelings for the ski lodge? For Jack? What was she so afraid of?

She dragged her thoughts back to her plan, hoping to see the secret lover again—this evening.

JACK COULDN'T SIT STILL. He had time to kill and too much on his mind. He kept thinking about Denny and Liz. It beat worrying about Karen and fuming in frustration that he didn't know where Baxter had her.

Denny had said he'd met Liz at the Oxford for a drink. Jack doubted that, even if the same bartender was on duty, he'd remember Denny and Liz, but it was worth a shot.

The bar, locally known as The Ox, was only a few blocks away. The walk felt good, the day warm and clear, but not hot yet.

Jack pushed open the door to find the bar half-empty this time of the day. Fans turned overhead against the dark green of the old tin ceiling. He pulled up one of the red vinyl stools and sat down. Behind the bar, a variety of old rifles were framed in glass and wooden boxes. He studied them until the bartender slid a napkin in front of him and asked what he'd take.

The bartender was a robust blond woman who fortunately was friendly. He engaged her in conversation. About the spring weather, the University of Montana Grizzlies' basketball season and finally the murder at the Carlton.

"You know that woman was in here the other night with some guy," the bartender said.

Always skeptical, Jack asked, "You remember her, huh?"

"Can't help but remember her. She was with this really good-looking guy." Denny. "But the only reason I remember her was the fight she got into with him."

The blood pounded in Jack's ears. "Do you know what they were fighting about?"

She laughed. "Probably the usual. Another man. I

only caught the worst of it and it sounded like she'd done something to really tick him off. He kept saying, 'How could you do something like that to me? What the hell did you think was going to happen when I found out? I could kill you with my bare hands for doing this to me.'''

Jack felt sick. He left a large tip and stumbled out into the spring afternoon, afraid Denny wouldn't show back at Al and Vic's, let alone bring him Karen's location. And it was less than twenty minutes until the second meeting.

Jack tried to put the picture together. Liz and Denny. The married woman Denny had been seeing on the sly? Didn't seem likely since Liz supposedly had only been in town a week. But Columbia Falls wasn't that far away. They could have been meeting for some time.

Add to that, the fight at the bar. Over another man? Liz's secret lover? The woman had more secrets than the CIA. Then Denny gets wind of it and blows. The next thing you know Liz is dead. Jack didn't like the way it all fell into chronological order.

The question was how long did the secret lover stay in Liz's room? What if he'd left quickly and Denny had been waiting in the wings? There were thirty-five minutes between the moment when Karen had seen Liz open the hotel room door to the mystery man until the time when Liz was murdered. A lot could happen in thirty-five minutes.

Too much. Had Denny been the one who called Karen after Liz was dead? Had he been the one to find Liz's latte shop napkin with Karen's number on it? It had been Denny's idea for Karen to put the newspaper ad in the personals column, knowing Karen would be risking her life.

With a terrible sense of foreboding, Jack went back to the first bar to wait for Denny, praying his friend would show. Praying he was wrong and that there was another explanation.

DENNY DIDN'T SHOW when he was supposed to. Jack was sipping a beer, growing more anxious, when a news special flashed on the television.

"Could you turn that up?" he asked the bartender.

"Dr. Carl Vandermullen had been picked up for questioning by police and released, following the murder of his ex-wife Liz Jones," the newsman said. "Their divorce was finalized just twenty-four hours before Jones was found murdered at the Hotel Carlton. Dr. Vandermullen refused to comment except to say his ex-wife's death was a great loss and he hopes the police apprehend the killer soon."

Baxter had obviously used kid gloves on the doctor.

Regular programming resumed and Jack looked again at his watch, growing more anxious as the clock ticked away each minute. The second meeting was to go off in less than ten minutes. But Denny had no reason to be there. He'd been taken off the case. And he knew Karen wasn't going to be there.

So where was Denny? Had he found Karen's hiding place and gone there instead? Had Jack just enlisted the killer to find Karen?

Denny walked in just as Jack was getting ready to leave.

"Baxter's got her locked up tighter than hell and

no one is talking, and I mean no—'' Denny stopped in midstep, midsentence. ''What is it?''

''Dammit, Denny,'' Jack cursed. ''I know about the fight you had with Liz the night you met her for a drink, just two days before she was killed.''

''Don't do this, old buddy.''

''Where's Karen?'' he demanded.

''I don't know.'' Denny glared at him, anger in his dark eyes. ''I told you. I couldn't get squat.''

Jack shook his head. ''I need to know the truth, Denny. Now. No more bull.''

''I already told you I didn't have anything to do with Liz's death. I want her killer caught as much as you do. More.'' He looked away, then motioned to the bartender that he was going in the back and didn't want to be bothered.

''Get a clue,'' Denny said the moment they were seated at the farthest table in the back. ''Why do you think I called you Saturday morning and told you it was urgent that you come to the Carlton?''

''A stupid practical joke.'' Except it seemed all wrong considering what he now knew about Denny and Liz.

''Would I have wanted you on this case if I'd killed Liz?'' Denny demanded. ''Look, Jack, you're the best cop I know. That's why I need you.''

''Need me?''

''To help find this guy.''

''Then why have you been trying so hard to get rid of me?''

''Because I know you. You do just the opposite of what anyone tells you to. If I'd have acted like I wanted you on this case, you'd be up in the mountains right now. Fortunately for me, you're stubborn as hell and you met Karen Sutton.''

Maybe fortunate for Denny, Jack's meeting Karen, but Jack wasn't so sure it was fortunate for him. But he'd definitely gotten involved.

"Why?"

"I want Liz's killer," Denny said, his words hard, the humor of a moment ago, long gone.

Jack didn't like the vengeful look in his partner's eyes, but it definitely confirmed what he'd suspected. "She was your first love, the one you told me about.''

Denny put his elbows on the table and cupped his face in his hands. He looked tired and incredibly sad. "It was like what you said happened with you when you first saw Karen. Zap. I never thought I would ever love anyone the way I loved Liz.''

Jack waited, sensing more to Denny's story. A whole lot more.

"I get this call from her last week," Denny began slowly. "After all these years, she calls me out of the blue. Just hearing her voice—" He shook his head and looked out across the bar. "She says she needs to talk to me. So I meet her at the Oxford. She probably figures it's someplace her doctor husband doesn't frequent.''

Denny took a breath and let it out slowly. "I'd heard she'd married Vandermullen so I figure she either wants to rub it in about marrying a successful doctor, every girl's dream, or she's got marital problems and just wants a familiar shoulder to cry on and that's why she wants to see me." He scrubbed his hands over his face. "Then she drops the bomb-shell."

Jack stared at his friend, holding his breath, afraid to move a muscle. *God, don't let him tell me he killed her. For any reason.*

Denny's next words were so unexpected that Jack thought he'd heard wrong. "She told me we had a daughter." He shot a look at Jack. "Liz was pregnant when she broke up with me. Said she didn't know it at the time. She left town. Gave the baby up for adoption."

Jack didn't know what to say. Couldn't find any words for a few moments. He could see how hard the news had hit Denny. Much harder than Jack would've ever imagined.

"Why tell you now, after all these years," he asked finally.

"She'd been trying to find our daughter and had reason to believe she'd been adopted by a family in Missoula. She wanted my help. The adoption had been handled illegally."

Jack dreaded to think what kind of help Liz had solicited. "What did you do?"

Denny let out a bitter laugh. "Nothing. We got into a huge fight, as you know. I threatened to throttle her for keeping this from me. I was so angry—" he shook his head "—I just couldn't deal with it. It was bad enough that she'd torn out my heart when she dumped me, but this— I stormed out of the bar, try-ing to cool off. Liz left and I...followed her."

Jack didn't like the hole Denny was digging for himself. No wonder his friend hadn't told him or anyone else about this.

"I just had this feeling that she was lying to me about something. I couldn't put my finger on it."

"You didn't believe you'd had a child with her?" Jack asked.

"That was the *only* thing I did believe," he said. "Everything else about the story just didn't ring true, you know?"

Jack knew. Maybe that's why they'd become cops. Cynics with a sixth sense for bullpuck. And a need for justice.

"I followed her to the cemetery," he said. "I watched her from a distance as she knelt by a grave. She looked like she was crying. After she left, I went over to where she'd been kneeling and shone my flashlight on the gravestone." Denny swallowed, his eyes hardening.

Jack held his breath.

"It was the grave of a baby girl who'd died at birth on March 11, 1984. The same day Liz said our baby had been born. The baby's name was Joanna Kay."

Named after her father, Jack thought with a start. Johnny K. The name Liz had known Denny by. "I'm sorry," Jack said, not knowing what else to say.

Denny shook his head. "Liz had buried her in the Missoula City Cemetery, right there between Interstate 90 and the railroad tracks, just blocks from where I was raised, on the wrong side. Ironic, huh?"

The bitterness in his voice couldn't cloak the horrible hurt. To find out he'd fathered a child and only hours later learn that the baby had died at birth. Why had Liz done this to him?

"You realize that all of this only gives you more of a motive for killing her," Jack said, still a cop.

Denny smiled and nodded. "If I could have found her that night—"

Jack realized Liz seemed to have that effect on men. She made them want to kill her. Only now one of them had.

"Why would she tell me that she was searching for our daughter then go to her grave?" Denny said.

Jack shook his head. He'd never understood women. "Maybe she wanted to hurt you."

Denny let out a snort. "Well, she succeeded."

"But you still want to find her killer?" he said, a little surprised.

"Oh, yeah," Denny said. "Whoever killed her, killed any chance I had of learning the truth about my daughter."

"Then that night at the Oxford was the last time you saw Liz alive?"

Denny lit a cigarette, taking his time. "I saw her again. I followed her to the Carlton Saturday night, determined to get the truth out of her about my kid."

Jack groaned.

"Afraid so, old buddy. But I never talked to her. I ran into someone I knew and figured I could take it up with Liz later. I was wrong."

Chapter Ten

Getting away proved easier than Karen had anticipated. She guessed it was partly her face. Her father
used to say she had the face of an angel. Her mother
used to add, "But the mischief of the devil in her."

Whatever it had been, she was now clambering
down the fire escape.

She had only minutes to get across the river to the
carousel. Not nearly enough time to find a good place
to see and not be seen, but she'd have to wing it.

She knew she was taking her life in her hands and
that if she was caught again by Baxter and his men,
he would definitely demand the psychiatric evaluation. Only this time she wasn't so sure she could
convince the doctor she didn't have a death wish.

But it was a wish to live that sent her racing toward the city's carousel. As she ran, she had the feeling that she was being watched. At least her paranoia
was still alive and well. Except it wasn't paranoia
when someone really was trying to kill you, right?

With the sun low, it was almost cold out. She wondered where Jack was. If he still had a job. If she'd
ever see him again. The thought made her falter. Of

course, she'd see him again. Destiny had brought them together, hadn't it? Then destiny would bring them together again. If it *was* destiny. Shoot, dumb luck would be all right, too. Just so she got to see him again.

The carousel was housed in a carriage house beside the Clark Fork River. Only a few cars were in the lot since it was almost closing time for the ride. She could hear the band organ playing and see the colorful horses.

She wondered if the person who'd answered her ad was already inside. It seemed an odd place to meet. Too public and yet not public enough—especially if she was expected to ride on the revolving carousel.

She crossed the bridge and started down the stairs to river level, the carousel in sight. She hadn't descended but a few steps when she saw him. He was sitting in a car, not the large, dark sedan from before, but a smaller blue one parked under the Higgins Street bridge. He appeared to be watching the carousel.

Her heart banged against her ribs. She fought to catch her breath. She couldn't let him get away. Not this time. Frantically she looked around for a phone booth and spotted one past the carousel to the west. She would still be able to see the man from the phone booth as well as the hotel across the river and the bridge, just in case her two guards had discovered she was missing and were already looking for her.

She took the stairs at a run and, keeping to the shade of the buildings, hurried to the phone booth. She started to dial 911, then stopped herself. She didn't trust the police. Not after Baxter had had her locked up for her own good. She dialed Jack's cell phone number instead, praying he'd answer. Praying he wasn't in jail. Or worse—

She opened the phone booth door to let air in, feeling a little claustrophobic, turning her back to the man in the car as Jack answered.

"Jack!" she cried, ecstatic to hear his voice. "Jack, I found him!"

"Karen? Where are you?"

"In a phone booth by the carousel."

"How did you get away from the men guarding you? Never mind, it doesn't matter."

"Jack, I can see him. He's sitting in a car under the Higgins Street brid—"

The explosion drowned out everything, setting the sky on fire. Bricks and dust and flames showered down like fireworks across the river. For a few seconds Karen could only stare in disbelief.

"Karen? Karen? Are you still there?"

"The hotel, Jack, it blew up." No, not the hotel. Just the top floor. "Jack, the floor of the old hotel where they'd been keeping me. It just blew up."

She heard Jack swear. "Karen, I'm on my way. I'm just a few minutes away. Stay on the line with me."

She turned then to look back at the car under the bridge. The navy-blue car hadn't moved. But the man who'd been behind the wheel was gone. "Jack, he's—" She heard the crunch of gravel behind her and turned just in time to see the man from Liz's hotel room. In that instant, she realized what it was about him that had made her recognize him the second time at the hotel and again in the car. "Oh, God, Jack, it's—"

The blow to her head radiated pain, then stars, then blackness.

JACK TURNED ON his lights and siren, knowing that Captain Baxter would hear about this and he'd be fired if not thrown in jail. He didn't give a damn. He had to get to Karen and fast.

Karen had said she could see the man. Jack assumed she meant the man she'd witnessed with Liz at the Carlton the night of the murder. Sitting in a car under the Higgins Street bridge. Then something had exploded. The hotel where Baxter had hidden Karen. How could that be? And then the man was gone, Karen said.

But it was her last words that Jack couldn't get out of his head. "Oh, God, Jack, it's—"

It's what? And why had she stopped talking and the phone gone dead as if someone had hung it up?

He floored the Jeep around a corner just missing a UPS truck. Hadn't he known something was wrong? The second letter. It had only been a diversion, while the killer's real target was the hotel and Karen.

Karen said the floor she'd been on at the hotel had blown up. The killer had known where she was. Jack wondered how she could have gotten away. Not that he cared. He didn't question the gods of fate. Especially this time.

But had she walked into another trap the killer had set for her?

Just let her be safe.

The Jeep screamed around a corner. *Just let her be safe.* He repeated it in his head. A mantra. If he'd owned a rabbit's foot he'd be clutching it right now. He felt as if his entire future hinged on the next few minutes.

The Jeep roared under the Higgins Street bridge and screeched to a stop in clear view of the carousel and the phone booth. Across the river, black smoke boiled up from the top of some old brick hotel. He could hear the cry of sirens and smell the smoke, but all he cared about right now was the phone booth and the small crowd gathered around it.

He leaped out of the Jeep and ran toward the crowd, propelled by a fear that had his heart lodged in his throat.

The people parted to let him through and he saw her. She sat in the corner on the concrete floor, supported by the walls, her head tilted to one side, her eyes closed. She looked as if she'd fainted and simply slid down the phone booth wall.

He started to flash his badge but remembered he didn't have it. "I'm a police officer. Did anyone see what happened to her?" He could hear the band organ playing at the carousel. What had happened to all the cops who were supposed to be covering this stakeout?

"She was like that when I saw her," someone said.

Jack knelt down beside Karen and felt for a pulse. Strong and steady. Just like her, he thought with overwhelming relief. He felt her forehead. Cool and dry. That's when he noticed a bump the size of a golf ball on the side of her skull.

"Someone call an ambulance," he ordered.

"Already did. It's on its way," a voice from the onlookers informed him.

"I think she must have fallen and hit her head," someone else outside the booth said.

Jack doubted that. But he did think she'd been struck. By the killer?

A moment later Jack heard the sound of an ambulance drawing closer. Karen stirred in his arms. Her eyelids fluttered against her pale skin and he noticed how light her freckles were. She needed some sunshine on her face, he thought, and immediately thought of the ski lodge. He'd take her there. Take care of her.

But even as he thought it, he knew she'd be even more determined to find the person behind this herself. She'd been taken into protective custody, locked up and held by armed guards. Look at the chance she'd taken escaping to get to the carousel for the second meeting.

The fact that the killer had blown up a floor of the hotel and almost killed her in a phone booth wasn't going to slow her down. Just the opposite. And he knew there was nothing he could say that would dissuade her. Not this woman. Not this time. She wouldn't believe anyone could protect her now.

Her eyes opened. Aquamarine with flecks of gold.

"Hello," he said softly, never so glad to see those eyes looking at him. Even if she *was* frowning.

"How are you feeling?" he asked.

"My head hurts." She tried to sit up. The effort made her wince.

"Easy. Stay still. An ambulance is on its way."

She blinked. "Ambulance? What happened?"

"You don't remember?" he asked.

"No." She glanced around in confusion. "I don't remember...."

"Don't worry, I'll take care of everything until you're feeling better. If you'll let me do that," he added, bothered by the fact that she was still frowning at him.

"Do I know you?"

"Jack," he said studying her intently. "Jack Adams." The name didn't seem to ring any bells. "Do you know what day it is?"

"Of course. Friday, March 17."

Friday. The day before the murder. The day before she ran into Liz on the street and went to the coffee shop for some girl talk. The day before she became the only witness in a murder case.

"Where am I?" She frowned as if she realized she wasn't in the part of the town she thought she was. He felt her pull away. Friday. They hadn't met yet. He was a stranger. His heart sank.

She was still in grave danger and yet she didn't know it. Didn't remember anything—especially the face of the killer. Nor Jack Adams's face, he reminded himself. If he thought she wouldn't let him protect her before, she *really* wasn't going to now. Not a complete stranger.

The ambulance pulled in, lights flashing. An EMT ran toward the phone booth. In a few seconds Karen would be gone. Once she got into the ambulance headed for the hospital, Captain Baxter would hear about it. Jack knew he wouldn't be able to get near her after that. But the killer might. Look how close he'd gotten this time.

"Karen, you have to listen to me—"

She drew back, squinting at him as if trying to put him into focus. "Do I know you?" She didn't sound as though she'd necessarily mind knowing him.

The notion came out of nowhere. It never even hit idea stage. Certainly couldn't have been considered a plan because given more time he would have realized just how flawed it was. But he didn't have time. The words just popped out, almost of their own accord.

"Of course you know me, Karen. I'm your husband."

Chapter Eleven

Husband? She stared at the man. As in married? Surely she would remember getting married, wouldn't she?

He smiled. Jack Adams did have a nice smile and there *was* something about him—

"What have we got, Detective Adams?" an emergency medical technician asked from the open phone booth doorway.

Detective Jack Adams? She'd married a cop? She hated to consider what her mother must think of that.

"She fell and hit her head," her husband answered.

Is that what had happened? Could explain her headache and the fact that she and her husband were on the cold floor of a phone booth with a crowd outside and an ambulance waiting.

"How long have we been married?" she asked her cop husband quietly.

"Just a few...hours."

A few hours? He had to be kidding. She glanced down half expecting to find herself still in her wedding gown. "Was it an informal wedding?" she asked, trying to understand what she was doing in jeans, a T-shirt and sneakers.

"We eloped. Got married at city hall."

"Well, congratulations," the EMT said as her husband moved out of the way to let the man check her over.

She leaned back against the glass wall, feeling a little light-headed and confused and...married, she thought, looking over at Jack. His gaze met hers and she felt something chemical arc between them.

"Wow, her pulse just spiked," the EMT said. "So did her heart rate."

She didn't doubt it. But after all, she was a newlywed.

The EMT shone a flashlight into her eyes. "Doesn't look like she suffered a concussion, though." He checked her vitals again. "She seems stable."

Stable? Karen doubted her mother would agree. "Have I told my mother yet?" she asked Jack. Jack. She liked the name. Jack Adams. A strong name. Just like him. Broad shoulders. Nice slim hips. She noted the way his jeans fit his behind. Ummm.

"No," Jack answered. "You wanted to wait."

Probably just wanted to put it off, she thought.

"Do you want us to take her in?" the EMT asked.

"No, I'll get a doctor to look at her," Jack said, studying her with concern.

She smiled. What a thoughtful husband she had. "I'm sure I'll be fine. How bad could a little fall be anyway?"

Her husband didn't look convinced. Husband. She thought she could get used to this.

"I'll take her to my doctor's office on the way," he said.

On the way where? "Are we on our honeymoon yet?" she asked, wondering how she'd hit her head in a phone booth and what the two of them had been doing here to begin with. Maybe he'd brought her to the carousel for a ride. She could hear the music and smell the river. What other reason would they be here?

Shouldn't they have been headed for some place more…intimate? At the least, more private than a phone booth?

But then she couldn't imagine herself married. Let alone eloping. Or getting married at city hall. Her mother was going to kill her.

"It isn't much of a honeymoon so far, huh?" she said as Jack helped her to her feet and over to a Jeep, the lights on top flashing red and blue. He really *was* a cop. "I'm sorry."

He closed the Jeep door and looked down at her through the open window. "You have nothing to be sorry about." He smiled then, a sweet, slow smile that warmed his eyes and sent a shiver through her.

Well, one thing she wasn't sorry about, she thought, as she watched him go around to the driver's side and climb in. She was pretty sure she was glad she'd fallen in love with this man.

"It must have been rather sudden," she said as he drove away from the river, the sound of the carousel fading away.

He nodded. "Love at first sight."

"I guess!" she said studying his face. She could see how it might have happened. He had a nice face, boyish but just imperfect enough to be interesting as well as masculine and definitely handsome.

But still, it seemed so unlike her. She had a feeling she hadn't been acting herself lately.

But what made her believe him was the electricity she felt sparking between them, especially when their gazes met and held.

Like right now. He'd looked over at her, concern still in the depths of his brown eyes. She felt herself sizzle under his gaze and smiled shyly. They must have a great sex life. She couldn't wait to have her memory refreshed.

"I want you to see a doctor, just to make sure you're all right," he was saying.

"I really am fine, Jack." She liked the feel of his name on her lips. "I don't want a silly little fall to spoil our honeymoon. Where are we going for our honeymoon?"

"It's a surprise."

"I love surprises," she said, sitting back in the Jeep and watching the world rush by. Married. It felt strange, but good. It felt unfamiliar, but somehow right. Just like this man beside her.

JACK PACED outside the doctor's examining room like a man in one of those old movies whose wife was about to give birth. When the doctor finally came out, he gave Jack a big smile and a slap on the back.

"Karen tells me the two of you were married this morning," he said. "Congratulations."

"Thank you," Jack said, knowing he was going to live to regret his impetuousness—and probably very soon. "How is she?"

"She has a slight concussion. I'd keep an eye on her."

That's exactly what Jack planned to do.

"And don't worry, her injury won't interfere with your honeymoon plans," he said with a wink.

Great, Jack thought as Karen came out of the examining room and he led her out to the Jeep. She took his arm. He could feel her body heat, warming the mild spring afternoon. He could feel himself begin to heat up as well. How was he ever going to be able to keep his distance from this woman?

"Tell me how we met," Karen said as he drove out of town. "Tell me everything."

"Wouldn't you rather wait until your memory comes back on its own?" he asked.

"No," she said cuddling next to him. "I want to hear your version, then when I remember, I'll know how we both felt. It really *must* have been love at first sight. I just can't imagine me doing something so…"

"Impetuous?" he supplied. It was going around.

She smiled and nodded. "I've always been so prudent and cautious. You must have really swept me off my feet."

Prudent and cautious? That definitely didn't fit the woman he'd come to know.

"You must bring out another side of me I didn't even know existed."

He groaned, afraid that just might be the case. Imagine what side he'd bring out in her when she got her memory back. The murderous side.

"Please tell me everything, from the moment we met to how we fell in love to the wedding ceremony and how I ended up in a phone booth on my honeymoon with a knot on my head.'' She ended with a laugh. ''Don't leave out a single detail.''

''Well,'' he began, wondering just where to begin and how much to tell her. Since the whole marriage was nothing but a lie, he could have made up any story he liked.

But instead, he found himself telling the truth. Up to a point.

''I literally could not take my eyes off you the first time I saw you,'' he began.

''LIZ JONES,'' Karen said, shaking her head as they left Missoula far behind. ''How strange after all these years and how awful.''

He'd had to tell her about the murder. Wasn't any way to get around it. Just as he'd had to tell her about the man she'd seen in the hotel hallway. The man who had seen her and Jack's fear that she might be in danger.

She smiled and snuggled against him. ''I know it must not seem odd to you—it certainly does to me—but I feel so safe with you and I don't really remember you.'' She looked up into his eyes then, her expression serious. She seemed to study him for a very long time. ''I *do* know you,'' she said after a moment. ''Maybe not in my head but definitely in my heart.''

Guilt twisted at his insides. He almost told her the truth right then. He knew by lying about the marriage he had only compounded the problem. But if he hoped to keep Karen alive, he had to protect her not only from the killer but the police. He had to con-

sider that there was a leak in the department. Or that
Baxter had gotten sloppy when he stashed Karen on
the top floor of the hotel. And where had all the cops
been at the second stakeout?

Whatever was going on, he couldn't trust the police to take care of her.

Karen loved the ski lodge and the view, just as she
had the first time. Only now, in what was left of
daylight, she wanted to explore the place, including
the old chalet. He had to smile at her delight at finding the chalet stuffed with old furniture and odds and
ends. She was full of ideas on what they could do to
restore the place and live in it full-time, and he listened to her, caught up in her excitement. But he
knew once she found out the truth, all of those ideas
would be tossed out like yesterday's newspaper—
along with him.

"Jack, I know something is bothering you," she
said, later back at the lodge. "Are you having regrets
about...us?"

He looked over at her, her eyes large and filled
with anguish. He quickly shook his head, his gaze
softening at just the sight of her. This woman had
the ability to turn him to mush with just a look. Or
turn him as hard as titanium with a whole other look.

"I could never regret meeting you," he said, realizing just how true that was. "You are the most
amazing thing that has happened to me."

She smiled, tears welling in her eyes. "Oh, Jack."
She rushed into his arms. He held her, wondering
how something so wrong could feel so right.

"What did the doctor say about..." Her eyes were

large, her gaze so filled with love—and desire—as she pulled back to look at him.

He swallowed, feeling like the lowest form of animal life. Wasn't he the one who was always telling Denny that one lie led to another until you were caught up in them like a net?

Well, Jack was caught. And badly. But what other option did he have? Return her to Baxter and let him put her in another safe house? Not after the last one had blown up. Not after someone had tried to kill her a third time at the phone booth.

No, the only way Jack could protect her was to keep her with him and keep up the pretense a little longer. He'd done the chivalrous thing. Right?

"The doctor said we should wait because of your head injury," Jack told her.

Disappointment clouded her expressive eyes. "I'm sorry. You must be as disappointed as I am."

She had no idea. Just the mere thought of making love to her... Disappointment didn't even cover what he was feeling.

Then she smiled. "But I suppose we have the rest of our lives."

He saw her glance down at her ring finger on her left hand as if a little surprised and...disappointed to find it bare. She probably thought she didn't have a very caring or romantic husband.

"You're probably hungry," he said, feeling like an even worse heel.

"Actually, I'm not," she said, right behind him.

He glanced back at her. "I picked up some doughnuts. Lemon-filled."

She shook her head. "We must have a very passionate relationship," she persisted.

He felt his heart skip a beat at the thought. "What makes you think that?" he asked with a nervous laugh.

She laughed, too, hers more natural, though. "When I'm around you I feel...sparks." She shrugged. "I've never felt like this around anyone else."

He definitely knew what she meant.

"And when I look at you, it's like the rest of the world doesn't exist." She shrugged, her smile bright as any summer day he'd ever seen. "You probably think that's silly."

"Not at all," he said, his voice cracking.

"And when I touch you—" She placed the flat of her hand against his chest, directly over his heart.

Oh, God. He closed his eyes, his heart a sledgehammer. Oh, yeah. He opened his eyes to find her gaze on his.

"Good," she said laughing, sounding relieved. "I'm glad I'm not the only one who feels this way. It certainly explains why we got married the way we did, huh?" She slid her hand up his chest and along his shoulder to his arm, then pulled back slowly as if reluctant to break the connection. "But there is something I was wondering about."

He held his breath.

"It's such an old-fashioned thing for us to do, getting married instead of just living together first," she said. "I have a feeling you're the one who insisted on marriage. Such a gallant kind of thing to do."

Yeah, gallant. Really heroic. But he *was* relieved

that was the only thing bothering her. "When I met you," he said honestly, "you just reminded me of my image of the Girl Next Door. I wanted you almost the first time I saw you." It shocked him how true that was.

"Oh, Jack, that's so romantic," she said, throwing her arms around his neck.

He circled her slim waist with his arms and hugged her to him, the feel of her an intoxicant that made him light-headed—and aroused.

She pulled back to look into his eyes. "I can't wait until I can remember every minute of it."

Yeah, he couldn't either. The doctor had said her memory loss would be short-term. The question was, how short-term? When she remembered maybe she'd be able to tell him who the killer was. But she would also remember that they weren't married. Not even close. That she didn't need him. And would now know that he had lied and couldn't be trusted. The thought made him sick inside.

"In the meantime, you have time to take a nice hot bath before dinner," he suggested.

She smiled, her eyes an inviting blue. He knew better than to go there. "I wish you could join me in the tub," she said suggestively. Nor there, especially.

His Girl Next Door was turning out to be quite the woman. More of a woman than he'd imagined, that was for sure.

"Yeah, I wish I could, too," he said, meaning every word of it.

He waited until he heard the water running in the tub, before he called Denny from his cell phone.

"What the hell happened at the safe house?" he demanded when Denny answered.

"I've been trying to reach you."

Jack had turned off his cell phone, busy trying to figure out how to deal with the latest challenge—his new bride.

"Where is Karen?" Denny demanded.

Jack had a sudden clear mental picture of her in the claw-foot bathtub. He dragged himself back from the enticing scene of his "wife" chin-deep in a bubble bath. "I don't know." Another lie. All for a good cause.

"I don't believe you," Denny said, no recrimination in his voice. "You'd be freaking out if you didn't."

Freaking. The same word Liz had used on the answering machine tape. "This is so freaky."

"At least she wasn't in the hotel when it blew up," Denny said.

"She was determined to go to the meeting place so she gave her guards the slip."

"Amazing woman, isn't she?"

More than Denny knew. "There has to be a leak in the department," Jack said, voicing his suspicions.

"Seems that way, huh?" Denny was silent for a moment. "I hope you don't think I had anything to do with it."

Silence. Jack didn't know what he thought anymore.

"Baxter is going crazy," Denny warned. "He's beside himself. I thought he was going to shoot the two officers who lost her."

"They got off the floor before it exploded?" Jack asked in surprise.

"Supposedly, they were out looking for Karen. It seems she climbed out the bathroom window while they thought she was taking a bath, and down a fire escape."

Jack shook his head and smiled to himself. "She's something, that's for sure."

"Yeah, well, Baxter wants her found," Denny said.

"Denny, there weren't any cops at the stakeout. Someone had pulled them off."

"I heard Baxter got a call that said Karen was in trouble at the hotel and they were responding when it blew up."

Is that where they'd been, just across the river when Karen was attacked? How convenient. Jack no longer knew what to believe.

"Another letter came to the paper," Denny said into the silence.

Jack wasn't surprised. The killer had failed twice. He wanted another chance. Especially now with Karen missing. "When is she supposed to meet with this one?"

"Tomorrow night."

Jack knew he should tell Denny about Karen's memory loss. This was his partner. But he couldn't trust even Denny. Not now. Not until he could prove to himself that Denny wasn't involved.

"Who knows what Baxter will do if he can't locate Karen before then," Denny said. "You think it's another setup." It wasn't a question. Denny had to be thinking the same thing Jack was.

"Yeah. I think all the killer really wants is to draw her out now. He doesn't care if she's made him—or if she's told anyone else what she knows. He just wants her dead. With her dead, it would be hard to prove he killed Liz."

Denny was silent.

"How are you holding up?" Jack asked.

"All right."

He didn't sound all right.

"That new cop, Marni Phillips, is about Karen's size," Jack said. "Baxter could have her fill in tomorrow night and see who shows."

Jack heard the water draining in the bathroom. Karen would be coming out soon. The thought of her fresh from the tub, her skin rosy and glowing set a fire in his groin.

"I have to go," he told Denny and turned to find her standing barefoot, her body wrapped in his robe, her damp hair a dark fringe around her glowing face. How much had she heard? The look in her eyes said, *enough.*

KAREN STARED at her husband, touched by what she'd heard of the conversation. The killer was still on the loose but another man had responded to the ad Jack had told her she'd put in the newspaper. Another meeting had been set. But Jack wanted a female cop to take her place.

"I should be there," she said softly.

He looked a little surprised, then shook his head. "Too dangerous."

"You say you think there's a leak in the police

department," she reasoned. "Unless I really show up, then neither will the killer."

He laughed. "Your logic has always scared me."

"That's probably because it's so…logical," she said, laughing as she moved closer. Oh, how she wanted him to make love to her. Forget what the doctor had said. Throw caution to the wind. Just take her, madly, passionately.

No, she was definitely not herself. But she liked this new her. And thought she could get used to her. And Jack.

"Jack, I feel so good—" She pressed closer and trembled as her gaze met and held his. "Don't you want to live dangerously?" She saw the answer in his eyes.

He took her upper arms in his large hands and pulled her closer. She thought he planned to kiss her. She knew by the look in his eyes that once he did, he wouldn't be able to stop. They would finally be true honeymooners. She could hardly wait.

But instead of a kiss, he whispered, "Believe me, ever since I met you, I've been living dangerously. More than you know." He swatted her on the behind and moved away from her. "Forget it, Karen. We're going to follow doctor's orders. I refuse to risk your health for—"

She followed his gaze to find that his robe had fallen open exposing a fair amount of her naked body beneath.

With a groan, he headed for the bedroom. "I'm going to get you something to wear."

She smiled after her cop husband. That definitely was not a gun in his pocket.

After she'd dressed in jeans and a sweater—what she'd discovered in her suitcase definitely wasn't much of a trousseau—she found Jack sitting in front of the fire, a frown on his face. She'd glimpsed that same worried look earlier.

"What is it, Jack?" she asked as she joined him on the couch. She curled up next to him and he put his arm around her as if he'd done it a thousand times before. "Is it something you can talk to me about?"

He seemed to hesitate. "It's this friend of mine, actually my partner...." He told her about Liz's bombshell she'd dropped on Denny, about the trip to the grave, about Liz lying about searching for the baby.

When he'd finished, she didn't say anything for a few moments, just sat thinking to herself. "Keeping a secret like that..." she said finally. "Can you imagine what a burden it would be to live a lie that many years? Poor Liz. But I can understand how your friend Denny must feel."

She mulled over everything she'd learned about Denny, Jack, Liz and herself over the days she'd lost. A lot of what she'd heard surprised her. For a woman who seldom got away from her workbench, she'd certainly gotten into a lot of trouble and involved with some interesting people. Jack especially. "The baby is the key," she said emphatically.

He pulled back and seemed to study her as if surprised. "Why do you say that?"

"Because, why would she pretend to look for a baby she knew was buried at the City Cemetery?"

"Maybe she wasn't in her right mind, after the divorce and all," he suggested.

Karen shook her head. "From what you've told me, she was nervous when I had coffee with her. She was upset when I saw her at the hotel with the man in the hallway. And she left me a message on my answering machine indicating she'd found out some things about the man she'd been seeing that had made her angry."

Jack nodded as if all those things would have led him to believe Liz was unstable.

"She sounds like a woman in trouble. I'd try to find out what happened to the baby," she said. "Isn't that what Liz said she was trying do before she was killed?"

Jack laughed. "Yeah, it was." He drew back to look at her, fascinated by this woman. There was so much more to her than he'd ever imagined when he'd first seen her in the hotel lobby—and he'd been captivated by her even then. "I think you just might have something." The baby definitely added a different dimension to the case. If it was dead, then there would be paperwork, proof. If not... He smiled at her. "You are something else."

She smiled back at him, her eyes warming, her gaze starting a fire in him. "Isn't that why you married me?"

Her words were like a bucket of ice water. He got up and moved away, his right side imprinted with the feel of her.

"What's wrong?" Karen asked behind him.

"This is very hard for me," he said, ready to tell her the truth and suffer the consequences. He hated lying to her. He hated seeing love and trust and desire in her eyes and knowing that it was all a lie.

"Oh, Jack, I'm sorry. I know you want me as much as I want you."

She thought this was about sex?

"I'm not being fair, asking you to make love to me, when all you're trying to do is protect me," she said.

That much was true at least.

His cell phone rang. Damn, he'd forgotten to turn it off. He'd expected to hear Denny's voice. Or even Baxter's. The one voice he hadn't anticipated hearing was Janet Henderson's.

"Jack?"

He felt his heart quicken at the ex-cop's tone. "Janet, what is it?"

"It's Denny. He's been mugged."

Mugged?

"He's in the hospital. He asked me to call you. He said if he called, you wouldn't believe him."

Just Denny crying wolf again. "How badly is he hurt?"

"He's been beaten up pretty bad. He'll be laid up for a while. But I think he's in some mess other than the mugging."

At least *that* Jack believed. A coincidence that Karen had been attacked? Then Denny? Both on the same day? Both within hours of each other? Jack thought not.

"No one else knows about this," Janet was saying. "He'd like to keep it that way. He's in room 204."

Was Denny afraid that whoever had done this would come after him in the hospital? That didn't sound like Denny. But who knew just how much trouble he was in?

Jack looked over at Karen. Her eyes were wide with concern. He couldn't leave her here alone. Especially on their honeymoon. "We'll be right there," he told Henderson.

Chapter Twelve

They entered through the back way of the hospital. Jack wasn't surprised to find an old high school friend of Denny's sitting outside his room.

The large man Jack knew only as Bruno the Biker stood as they approached and Jack felt certain Denny would be safe with this man standing guard.

"He wasn't sure you'd come," Bruno the Biker said.

"Sure he was," Jack said and shook the man's hand. Bruno studied Karen for a moment, taking her measure. "This is Karen." Jack hesitated. "My wife."

Bruno lifted a brow, smiled and nodded. "Nice."

"Thanks," Jack said and quickly ushered Karen into Denny's room.

Denny looked as white as the sheets on his hospital bed. A bandage hid most of his dark hair, but his dark eyes missed nothing as Jack and Karen entered.

"You remember Karen," Jack said quickly.

"Hard to forget."

"I'm sorry I don't remember you," she said, extending her hand.

Denny took her hand with a frown, his gaze shifting to Jack's. Jack could tell it hurt Denny to move his head.

"It's a long story," Jack said in answer to the look. "How are you?"

"Hell of a headache, but other than that... I got to thinking after I talked to you. It just didn't add up. So I did a little digging. I found Liz's ad, the one she ran in the personals last week. I had it in my pocket, but whoever hit me took it and my wallet and left me for dead."

"Most muggers aren't interested in personal ads," Jack commented.

Denny smiled. "My feeling exactly."

"What did the ad say?" Karen asked.

"It was short and sweet. 'On March 11, 1984 I saw you take her. I saw you again yesterday. You recognized me, too. Contact me at once or suffer the consequences.' Liz always did have a way with words."

So the ad hadn't been about finding a lover, secret or otherwise. Maybe Liz really *had* been looking for her baby.

"Now that I think about it, Liz never said she was *sleeping* with the man," Karen said thoughtfully. "She said she had a 'relationship' with the mystery man. I guess I just assumed he was a lover. Why else had she advertised for him in the paper?"

Jack stared at Denny. Had Liz's search always just been for her child? Had the man she met that night at the Carlton been the man who had Denny's daughter?

"Jack told me about the baby," Karen said, moving closer to his bed. "You think the mystery man is the connection to your daughter?"

Denny nodded. "March 11, 1984 was our daughter's birthday. I think she's alive. And he knows where."

Jack worried that Denny and Karen were reading too much into the ad. Mostly, he just hated to see his friend get his hopes up. "If that's true, then we should be able to find proof. There will be paperwork to prove it one way or the other."

Denny shook his head. "I already checked. Joanna Kay Vandermullen was born on March 11, 1984 at 1:57 a.m. and was pronounced dead a few minutes later. I found both a birth certificate and death certificate filed at the county courthouse. There is even a record of the purchase of a cemetery plot and a headstone—all signed by Dr. Carl Vandermullen."

End of story. So, why didn't he believe it any more than Denny did? Jack frowned. "What are you saying?"

"It was a home birth." Denny closed his eyes for a moment. When he opened them Jack didn't like what he saw there. "Vandermullen had to be in on it."

"In on what?" Jack demanded.

"I don't know," Denny admitted. "But I don't think the baby's dead. I think Liz was actually telling the truth. She was looking for our daughter. I think that's what got her murdered."

"Why would anyone murder her over an adoption?" Jack asked.

"To cover up what they'd done," Karen piped in. "If Denny is right, then Liz and Carl had wanted the world to believe their baby was dead. But at least one other person, the man Liz saw with her baby, knows the truth. I would imagine neither man wants that truth coming out now."

Jack shook his head. He should have known not to bring her. Didn't he realize she'd get involved in this? Hell, she was already involved. She'd seen the man with Liz. Whoever he was.

"Think about it, Jack," Denny argued. "The baby was born here. Liz met Vandermullen just weeks after breaking up with me, married him and moved to Columbia Falls."

"But Vandermullen kept his house here up in Rattlesnake," Jack pointed out.

"All right," Denny said. "Maybe Liz came back to Missoula to have the baby, hoping Vandermullen wouldn't realize how far along she'd been when she met him. Maybe he followed her. For some reason, she had a home birth."

"Did you ever think she might have come here to tell you about the baby?" Karen suggested.

That stopped them both. Denny stared at her. It was obviously something he hadn't considered. Nor had Jack.

All of it was just speculation, but he had to admit, a lot of it did make him wonder.

"Maybe Vandermullen never even knew the baby was mine," Denny said.

Jack stared at the two of them, a bad feeling in his gut. "Or maybe Vandermullen *did* know."

They both turned to look at him.

"You think this Dr. Vandermullen wouldn't have wanted the baby if he'd found out it wasn't his?" Karen asked. "That he made her give it up for adoption? Illegally, to hide the truth?"

Jack shrugged. He'd heard a little about Vandermullen. Enough to think that could have been the case. "Look, for all we know the baby died at birth. No mystery." That didn't, however, explain Liz's ad but then he wasn't sure any of them could explain Liz's last days let alone hours. They may never know what happened.

"Oh, Jack, the man Liz met at the hotel could be the mystery man she saw with her baby," Karen said. "If he is and the girl's alive, then he might know where she is."

"I think Karen's right," Denny said. "I think Liz got into more than the wrong bed."

Jack moaned. He was looking for Liz's killer. If she really had been looking for her child, then the two paths might have crossed.

"We may never know who that man was," he said to Karen. "Or where your daughter is—*if* she's still alive," he added for Denny's sake, hoping all the time that he was wrong about that.

His friend didn't say anything for a moment. Jack knew Denny had a plan and that he wasn't going to like it.

"You're probably right, Jack," he said finally. "But there is at least one person who knows the truth. Dr. Carl Vandermullen."

DR. CARL VANDERMULLEN had a large upscale home in Rattlesnake Canyon just minutes outside of Missoula.

Going anywhere near the doctor was a form of professional suicide that wasn't lost on Jack. Baxter would get wind of it. Although Missoula was the third largest city in Montana with a population of forty-three thousand, the entire state was like a small town when it came to the speed with which gossip traveled.

Bringing Karen along was an even worse plan. But low on options, Jack wasn't about to leave her unless he absolutely had to. At least with him, he knew she was safe. He also wanted to gauge Vandermullen's reaction when he saw her.

But the real reason Jack drove to the palatial home of the good doctor was for Denny. To find out what he could about the baby. And for Karen. There was still a killer out there who wanted her dead. If Vandermullen had any of the answers, Jack planned to get them.

As he pulled down the long stately drive into Dr. Vandermullen's, Jack looked over at Karen. She seemed quite happy sleuthing with him, even knowing her life was at risk. It startled him to realize it was because she trusted him. Worse yet, he liked it. Too bad he wasn't trustworthy, he thought as he parked the Jeep, cut the lights and sat for a moment waiting for his eyes to adjust to the dark.

A silver Mercedes convertible was parked in front of one of the three windowless garage doors. Jack wondered if a large, dark, newer American car was parked in one of the garages.

He'd borrowed Denny's gun and holster and felt less naked than he had since his recent suspension. But even with the pistol pressed against his ribs, he felt vulnerable. It was this case. It had taken too many twists and turns. At first he'd thought he was chasing a secret lover who'd killed Liz to keep her from ratting to his wife about their affair.

But now Jack wasn't sure who he was chasing or why. All he knew was that it felt more malevolent. More dangerous. And he felt more for Karen, a woman he feared was in worse danger than he knew.

"Ready?" he asked her softly.

She nodded and straightened, looking as if she were ready to take on evil single-handedly.

He smiled, realizing that the more time he spent around her, the more he liked her. She was sharp-witted, smart and entertaining company. His only concern, other than that fateful moment when her memory returned, was staying out of bed with her. The more time they'd spent together, the more Jack wanted her. Each hour, it was becoming increasingly difficult not to make love to her.

"Let's go," he said and climbed out to open her car door for her.

Vandermullen opened the large carved wooden door, dressed in slacks, a polo shirt and boat shoes. If he was surprised to see either of them, he didn't show it.

"Why, hello," he said, glancing from Jack to Karen, apparently recognizing them both. "And to what do I owe this honor?"

He sounded as if he might have had a few bour-bons but he didn't seem in the least antagonistic to find a cop and a star murder witness on his doorstep. His only reaction to Karen was to leer for a moment.

"We wanted to talk to you," Jack said. "In a strictly unofficial capacity."

"Well, then you'd better come in and have a drink," he said, seemingly amused, as he led them into a huge living room.

When Jack was seated on the couch beside Karen, the doctor took their drink orders. The air held the sweet distinct scent of bourbon and Vandermullen's glass had left a half-dozen wet ring marks on the glass coffee table.

Under normal circumstances, Jack would have declined a drink but he figured Vandermullen would feel more comfortable not drinking alone.

"Sure. Scotch if you have it. On the rocks." Jack looked to Karen.

"I'll take a beer," she said. "Bottle if you have it."

No white wine. Not even a lite beer in a glass. His Girl Next Door was just full of surprises.

Vandermullen seemed to find her choice of drinks delightful. He brought her a cold beer. "I assume you don't want a glass?" he said, smiling down at her.

Jack noticed that Carl Vandermullen wasn't a bad-looking man. Older, distinguished and in good shape, a man who would have no trouble finding another younger wife.

Karen smiled up at the doctor as she took the beer. "This is just perfect."

Jack watched her take a long drink, tilting her head

back, giving him a clear view of the pale vulnerable skin of her sleek neck.

Vandermullen stepped in front of him, blocking his view. He reached up to take the Scotch the doctor offered him, aware that Vandermullen had been flirting with Karen. Suddenly Jack wanted to nail Vandermullen for the murder and anything else he could dig up on him.

"So, what is it the two of you want with me?" the doctor asked, taking a chair across from them, a large glass of bourbon on ice in his hand. But when he spoke, his gaze went to Karen and stayed there.

Karen took a sip of her beer, trying to decide how she felt about the man. There was something too relaxed about him considering his ex-wife had been murdered and he'd been hauled down to the police department for questioning. But then, she reminded herself, he just might not have anything to hide. Or was a very good actor.

She glanced around the living room. Done all in white, it had the sterile feel of an operating room—except for several splashes of bright-red color tossed about the room like bloodstains.

"I know the police have already asked you, but I wondered what you were doing at the Carlton the night of Liz's murder," Jack said. "Also, what you were doing at El Topo yesterday afternoon?"

Vandermullen studied his bourbon for a moment. "I followed Liz to the hotel because I was worried about her." He looked embarrassed by the admission. "Liz always liked picking up strangers. She liked doing dangerous things like that. Going to bed with men she'd just met."

He shook his head sadly. "I followed her Saturday night because I knew she had a new lover. I could always tell. Only this one seemed...different. I feared he truly might be...dangerous."

Hindsight was twenty-twenty, Karen thought.

"I answered the ad for the same reason," he continued. "I knew Liz had met men through the personals columns before, so I guess I'd gotten in the habit of watching them, wondering who my wife would pick this time. When I saw your ad," the doctor said looking over at Karen, "I hoped you might know who'd killed her. No matter what happened between us, I want to see Liz's murderer brought to justice."

Neither Jack nor Karen said anything as he drained his glass and went to refill it. They both declined another drink. Karen wondered if Jack was surprised as she was that Vandermullen knew she'd been the one to put the ad in the paper. The only way he could have found out was from Captain Baxter.

It had also been clear when Vandermullen opened the door that he knew them both. Jack had told her that she'd seen Vandermullen at the Hotel Carlton. And he'd seen her. But had he also seen her at the El Topo, when according to Jack she'd almost been run down?

When Vandermullen sat back down again, he said into the silence, "I loved Liz, but the truth was, I couldn't keep her happy. Nor it seems could I protect her from herself."

He was trying to portray himself as the wounded husband who put up with his wife's infidelities because he loved her. Karen wished she could remember her meeting with Liz. Could Liz have been the woman her ex-husband was portraying her to be? Hadn't Jack told her that Liz had mentioned a jealous ex she'd recently left?

"Then you didn't see her at the Carlton Saturday night?" Jack asked. "Nor the man she met?"

Vandermullen shook his head. "The truth is, I realized it was over. I couldn't keep trying to protect her. Liz was on her own. Just the way she wanted it."

"Then you didn't hear about the murder until the next morning?" Jack pressed.

"No, not until the police called," he said, then seemed to mull over his thoughts for a moment. "I'm quite a bit older than Liz was. Maybe that was the problem."

"Or maybe it was losing the baby," Karen suggested, surprising them all, she noticed.

"Our daughter, Joanna?" Vandermullen exclaimed.

So he hadn't known that Denny was the baby's father? Or he did and wasn't admitting it? But it answered one question. There *had* been a baby at least. And it could have been Denny's.

"Why on earth would you want to know about the baby?" Vandermullen asked, sounding upset. "It's been more than sixteen years." He downed the rest of his drink and got up to pour himself another. "It was a tragic loss for us. Liz was devastated since she was unable to have other children."

"It was a home birth?" Karen asked.

Again Vandermullen looked surprised. "Why are

you asking about this now? I thought you were trying to solve her murder.''

Karen shrugged. ''I'm sorry, I just know that the baby was on Liz's mind. She'd mentioned the girl would be sixteen now. If she'd lived,'' Karen said, making it up as she went from what Jack had told her and what she and Denny suspected.

''Why would Liz mention the baby to *you?*'' Vandermullen asked, appearing shocked by that revelation.

''I assume because of the girl's birthday this month and maybe because Joanna Kay is buried here in Missoula,'' Karen said, noticing that she was making both Vandermullen—and Jack—uncomfortable.

''She told you a lot about…our daughter,'' Vandermullen said as he sat down again and took a drink. ''Yes, it was a home birth. It's what Liz wanted. She was deathly afraid of hospitals.''

''The baby died?'' Jack asked.

Vandermullen nodded. ''She was born with the umbilical cord wrapped around her neck.''

''How horrible,'' Karen said sympathetically. ''How was it that the baby was born here and not in Columbia Falls?''

Vandermullen's gaze locked on hers. ''This was Liz's hometown. She wanted her baby to be born here. Sentimental, I guess.''

''Probably the same reason she wanted your daughter buried here,'' Jack said, putting down his glass as he got to his feet. ''We really should be going. Thank you for your candor.''

Karen stood, wondering if the temperature in the room had dropped or if it was just her imagination.

"Anything to help you find Liz's killer," the doctor said, walking them to the door.

As THEY DROVE AWAY, Jack looked over at Karen. "Good work," he said. "Although you did make me a little nervous." More than a little nervous. She'd upset Vandermullen. With one woman already dead, Jack didn't like Karen upsetting the suspects.

Not that she wasn't already in danger. He just couldn't help feeling protective when it came to her.

Karen didn't answer. She seemed deep in thought. Probably thinking the same thing he was. About Denny's baby. How tragic for his friend. If only Liz had kept it to herself. What had she hoped to gain by telling him about Joanna *now?* It seemed so cruel. And it made Jack wonder if Liz *had* been in her right mind.

Not that he'd liked Vandermullen. Nor been sympathetic to the man's plight. But maybe it did give them a little insight into Liz in the hours before her death.

Maybe Vandermullen had been right to worry about his ex-wife. Her behavior was definitely bizarre. Telling Denny about a baby that had been dead for sixteen years. Hooking up with a complete stranger through a personal ad. Having a "relationship" with a man she knew nothing about—not even his name.

"He's lying," Karen said as Jack turned on Greenough.

"What?" he asked, swiveling his gaze to her.

"He's lying. Liz didn't hate hospitals. She worked as a candy striper in high school and wanted to be a nurse. I remember because it seemed at odds with a girl who ran with bikers and didn't show much interest in school. She used to borrow my notes in biology after skipping the class most mornings. I'd forgotten about that.'' Karen looked over at him. ''Does that sound like someone who was afraid of hospitals and wanted to take the chance of having her baby anywhere but in a hospital?''

He stared at her.

''If Vandermullen lied about that, then who says he didn't lie about the baby being born dead?'' she demanded.

''For what possible reason?''

''I know it's been sixteen years, but he didn't seem upset enough over losing the only child the two of them would ever have,'' she said. ''Maybe he knew the baby wasn't his. He was a doctor, for crying out loud. He could probably count up to nine months. Maybe he talked Liz into giving the baby up for adoption but to save face, let everyone believe it had died. Couldn't a man in his position fake a birth—and death—certificate?''

Her logic still scared him, but unfortunately often made a strange kind of warped sense. It fit Vandermullen. The kind of guy who'd only want his own kid with his own genes. Probably why they'd never adopted a child.

''You think Liz would go along with giving up her baby like that?'' Jack asked.

Karen shrugged. ''If she loved Vandermullen and knew he wouldn't accept her daughter for his own, yes. But she was bound to regret it. Maybe that's why she went to Denny with the truth. She wanted his help to find her daughter and make amends. She'd just divorced Vandermullen. It all ties together.''

Jack had to admit it did tie up pretty nicely. Maybe a little too nicely. "Why did she go to the cemetery, then, if she knew there was no baby buried there?"

Karen bit her lower lip in obvious contemplation. "Because, if I'm right, then the grave has been her only connection with her daughter for sixteen years."

Like a blade of ice, her words pierced his heart. He couldn't shake that image of Liz Jones beside her daughter's grave.

"Even if you're right, we have no way to prove it," he said, always the cop. "Liz is dead and Vandermullen is sticking to a completely different story."

"There has to be a way," Karen said, her voice full of determination. "The answer is in that grave."

He looked over at her. "Don't even say it."

"Jack, you know if I'm right, Vandermullen would never let us have the grave opened and any proof we might have been able to find probably died with Liz."

He stared at her. She couldn't seriously be considering— He swerved to keep the car on the road. Boy, had his first impression of this woman been off.

"Grave robbing is a felony, Karen, and I'm a cop." A cop on suspension, but still a cop.

"Then I'll do it myself," she said.

He glanced over at her again. "I can't let you do that." But he could tell by the look in her eyes that stopping her would be a whole other matter.

"Would you take me by my shop?" she asked sweetly. Too sweetly.

But how could he deny her such a simple request? He waited while she went into the back for a few minutes. She returned dressed in all black, carrying a bag that clunked suspiciously of tools.

"Karen—"

"Haven't you ever done something that you know is wrong, but you did it for the right reason?" she asked.

Oh, yeah.

Chapter Thirteen

Clouds scudded across the moon, dropping a cloak of darkness over the cemetery. Only a twinkling of stars lit the night sky. A breeze stirred the new buds on the deciduous trees and whispered in the tall evergreens as Jack boosted her over the six-foot-high chain-link fence that surrounded the silent graveyard.

Karen dropped onto the grass on the other side with a soft thud, then stood back as he tossed over the bag of tools. She couldn't help shivering at the sight of all the gravestones that glowed white as skeletons even in the darkness.

She watched Jack scale the fence and drop effortlessly beside her. He looked at her, his gaze questioning. It wasn't too late to turn back.

She shook her head slowly and glanced past him to the rows and rows of headstones. The mere thought of digging up the grave filled her with trepidation, but she believed in her heart that the answer to Liz's death was in this cemetery, buried in that baby's grave.

Just thinking about the baby unnerved her. What

if she was wrong? What if the baby really had died and Vandermullen was telling the truth?

No. He'd lied about Liz's fear of hospitals. He could have lied about the baby. Liz wouldn't have been looking for her child unless she believed Joanna Kay was alive.

Karen and Jack stood in silence for a long moment. As her eyes began to adjust to the darkness, she could make out the long line of railroad cars just across the road. On the other side of the cemetery, car lights flashed high on the hillside where Interstate 90 cut across the state.

IN THOSE FEW MOMENTS, Jack had time to contemplate the strange turn his life had taken since meeting his Girl Next Door. The irony of it didn't escape him.

His job was in serious jeopardy, he'd just interviewed a suspect in a case he wasn't supposed to be near, he'd lied about getting married and now he was standing in the cemetery in the middle of the night with a shovel.

He wondered if Karen had any idea what kind of effect she had on men. Or if he was just the lucky one.

Of course he'd argued that grave digging was illegal. That the thing to do was wait and try to get a court order to have the body exhumed. That grave robbing probably wouldn't be good for her after her accident.

But even as he'd offered excellent arguments, he could see he wasn't making a dent in her reasoning.

"You left out that it is probably morally wrong

and will make for very bad karma,'' she said when he'd finished, obviously not in the least dissuaded.

''Follow me,'' Jack whispered and picked up the tool bag. Denny had said the grave was on Hope, one of the narrow roads that wove through the dark cemetery.

Jack led the way through the maze of white headstones, expanses of dark grass and winding roads with names like Charity. Faith. And finally, Hope.

Following Denny's directions, he moved through the graves with Karen close behind. The moon broke free of the clouds. He stopped to get his bearings, feeling the steady thump of his heart inside his chest. God, he didn't want to do this.

But as he looked over at Karen he knew she was going to do it—with or without his help. And one way or another this would end any more speculation about why Liz Jones Vandermullen had come back to Missoula. And for him, it would answer a lot of questions about Liz herself.

Jack knew that if Liz really had been searching for her daughter, it was possible that's what had gotten her killed. It would definitely change Jack's approach to finding her killer—and keeping Karen safe.

But if Liz and Denny's daughter was in this small grave... Well, then he'd have to accept that Dr. Carl Vandermullen was telling the truth and that Liz had been killed by some stranger she'd picked up in the personals column.

As Jack neared the spot where Denny had said he'd find Joanna Kay Vandermullen's grave, he saw something even more unnerving. A shovel. It lay next to a gravestone ahead of them. It looked as if there were fresh dirt on the shovel.

As he and Karen stepped closer, Jack saw that someone had been digging up one of the graves. He knew before the moon cast its eerie light on the stone that it was Joanna Kay's grave.

The headstone was small and simple. Just the baby's name and date of birth and death. Jack felt a sliver of ice wedge itself in his chest. Someone else wanted to see what was buried here.

He glanced around, seeing no one, hearing nothing but silence. Not even a breeze whispered through the cemetery. Not even the rustle of a squirrel or a dried leaf. Nothing moved.

Jack looked over at Karen. She seemed paler in the moonlight, her freckles in stark contrast, her eyes wide and fearful. But her look was determined, even more convinced that they were on to something. It certainly seemed she was right.

He put down the bag of tools and pulled out a shovel. Slowly he began to dig where the last grave robber had left off.

THE TIME PASSED in a blur of moonlight and darkness. Earth spilled from Karen's shovel in hypnotic repetition. They hadn't spoken, just worked, neither wanting to talk about what they were doing or why. She suspected, like her, he feared they would find a small body in the grave. She didn't want to think what that would do to Denny. He wanted so desperately to believe his daughter was alive.

She'd tried to lose herself in the labor, avoiding thoughts of what they were digging up. Jack had argued she shouldn't shovel, but she'd won him over by assuring him she needed something to do.

She tried not to think at all, but thoughts scudded by like the clouds overhead. Mostly she thought of Jack, her heart welling with her love for him. Funny, but while she couldn't remember falling in love, she knew she had and obviously at first sight. Why else would she have agreed to marry him the way she had?

How odd to fall so desperately in love when so much was going on in her life. For so long, she'd lived a rather uneventful life. Now, according to Jack, not only had she fallen in love and gotten married, she'd become a witness in a murder case, been almost killed in a hit-and-run, and was now helping solve a sixteen-year-old mystery.

This was so unlike her. She hardly recognized herself. But, she had to admit, she was happier than she'd ever been. And Jack Adams was the reason. Being with him was definitely exciting in more ways than one.

Jack struck something with his shovel. He froze, his gaze coming to her.

She held her breath as he began to clear the dirt from around the small coffin so he could get the crowbar under the lid. She closed her eyes in a silent prayer, then opened them as she heard the sharp crack of the seal breaking.

"Hand me the flashlight," Jack whispered.

She did and watched the sphere of gold light fall across the tiny coffin. Jack seemed to brace himself, his gaze touching hers gently, then he lifted the lid slowly and shone the light inside.

He let out a curse.

She gasped, her hand going to her mouth. At first all she saw was a baby dressed in white. Then the light fell on the baby's face and she realized it was nothing more than a doll.

She felt tears rush to her eyes, unable to hold them back. No baby. Joanna Kay Vandermullen wasn't here. She bit her lip to hold back the avalanche of emotion as she looked down at Jack. Her heart surged with hope that the girl was alive.

He stood for a long moment, the flashlight hanging from his fingertips, his arm at his side, the circle of light glowing on the bottom of the grave. He didn't seem ready to climb from the hole. She wondered if he felt as sick inside as she did. He looked weak with relief and disgust. Someone had buried a doll in a baby's coffin. Someone had pretended that Joanna Kay had died at birth.

That someone had to be Dr. and Mrs. Carl Vandermullen. Did that mean that Liz *had* been searching for her baby? Is that what had gotten her killed? Had she found the mystery man she'd advertised for?

Or was Joanna Kay dead—just not buried here?

Jack clicked off the flashlight and climbed out of the hole. The moon disappeared behind a cloud, dropping a veil of darkness over them. Only a little light seemed to leak out over the mountains to the east.

They had to get out of here. Before the groundskeeper caught them. They had to tell Denny what they'd found. Joanna Kay could be alive.

Jack stuffed the tools into the bag. He picked up the bag then froze, his body alert. Karen heard it,

too. The unmistakable sound of a footfall. The faint
rustle of clothing. Just yards away, the clink of something brushing against one of the tombstones. Someone was out there. Hiding. Watching them.

Chapter Fourteen

Jack motioned for Karen to be silent although he could tell by the way she'd tensed next to him that she'd heard it, too, and was also trying to pinpoint where the noise had come from.

Could it be the groundskeeper getting an early start? Not likely. It was still dark outside. And the movement had been too...furtive. Too close.

He heard it again. The sound of clothing rustling as if someone had just shifted into a different position and it was close. Very close.

He heard a soft click and dropped the bag as he lunged to pull Karen down behind one of the larger gravestones.

The shot whizzed past, the bullet striking a tombstone behind them, sending up a spray of granite. The shooter had a gun with a silencer and wasn't a bad shot.

Jack pulled Denny's pistol from its holster. "Stay down," he ordered.

Karen nodded, her eyes wide with fear, her expression one of shock. Fortunately, Jack thought, she couldn't remember the other times someone had tried to kill her. Unfortunately, he could.

He stared at her for a moment, then impulsively, bent down to plant a kiss on her lips. She smiled and squeezed his knee, trust and love glowing in her gaze.

He glanced around, looking for a safe place for her. The hole they'd just dug loomed dark and deep. He motioned for Karen to slip back into the open grave. She didn't look ecstatic about the idea but she quickly complied without question.

A dream wife, he thought crazily, as he handed her the flashlight.

With Karen safe in the hole for the moment, he moved stealthily toward the direction he'd first heard the sound, his pistol drawn. Another shot zipped past with a hum, the bullet boring into a tree trunk behind him.

He rushed forward, using the gravestones for cover as he charged in the direction of the shot, determined to catch the killer, to stop him once and for all.

THE MOON FLASHED from behind the clouds, casting an eerie gray light over the cemetery. Down in the hole, the gray light only cast a long cold shadow.

Karen crouched, her body pressed against the damp earth, listening for Jack's return, fighting fear for her husband. She kept telling herself he was a cop. He knew what he was doing. He'd be all right.

She looked down at the coffin at her feet, fighting her own fears. The darkness, the cold earth, the moon eclipsed by the clouds overhead and that terrible feeling of helplessness. She shivered and tried to think of anything else but her fears.

She huddled in the dark of the grave and thought of Jack. What an odd way to spend a honeymoon. She hadn't even gotten to make love to her husband yet. And now they might both be going to jail. If they lived that long.

He had to come back to her. She couldn't bear the thought of losing him when she'd just found him.

As her eyes adjusted to the darkness in the hole, she realized that Jack had left the casket open. She could see the doll. She couldn't imagine someone putting a doll into the small box to be sealed and burying it, complete with headstone. It seemed so…sick.

She looked up at the clouds moving like waves overhead and listened for the sound of her husband returning. But she heard nothing down in the hole. Nothing but the frantic drumming of her pulse, her heart thundering in her chest.

Her gaze fell again on the coffin and the doll inside. The doll's eyes stared out, blank, but…familiar. She knelt down to inspect it more closely.

Pretty Patsy Wetsy, she thought with a start. She'd had a doll just like it.

Carefully, she reached in and started to lift the doll out, then jerked back with a muffled cry as she saw something that froze her blood.

JACK LET HIS EYES adjust to the moonlight. Exhaustion pulled at him. Weary from everything he'd learned, sick from all that he still didn't know or understand, he crouched behind a tombstone and

waited for the killer to make his move. He didn't
have to wait long.

A dark shape leaned out from behind one of the
mausoleums. The shot breezed by so close, Jack
thought it had grazed the side of his face. He ducked
back, breathing hard. He waited a few moments, tim-
ing it, then peered out again.

Nothing moved. Thin clouds sailed across the
moon, washing the cemetery in a ghostly white light.
Long shadows hid behind headstones and trees,
hanging on to the darkness.

Suddenly a furtive movement caught Jack's eye.
Someone ran out from behind one of the grave mark-
ers and now zigzagged through the pines and granite
headstones toward the chain-link fence, toward the
road and a large, dark car parked at its edge, a long-
barreled pistol in the shooter's left hand.

Jack leveled his gun, leaning across the top of the
gravestone, waiting for a shot. Just as the figure
reached the fence, he pulled the trigger. Boom. The
sound echoed across the graveyard, bouncing like a
pinball through the granite stones.

The would-be assassin seemed to hesitate for an
instant as if the bullet had found its mark. Jack had
shot only to wound the man. A leg shot. But as the
figure scampered up and over the fence, dropping to
the other side, Jack knew he'd erred on the side of
safety and had let the killer get away.

He took one more shot, knowing it was futile. Too
far to shoot for any accuracy. No chance of getting
closer before the person reached the car.

The bullet shattered the back side window of the
large, dark car as the driver leaped in. Jack heard the

sound of an engine roar to life and watched as the car sped away in a cloud of dust and gravel.

Jack swore as he holstered the pistol and ran back to the open grave—and Karen.

"Did you get him?" she asked in a whisper.

He shook his head. "I didn't even get a good look at him." Medium height, medium build, wearing a baseball cap. Driving a large, dark, American-made car. He could have been the man Karen had seen with Liz at the Carlton. He could have been anyone.

"You'll get him next time." She smiled up at him with a mixture of relief and love that was almost his undoing.

He offered her a hand up out of the hole and noticed she was holding something.

Her expression changed as she saw his gaze shift to the doll in her hands. "You aren't going to believe this, Jack."

She held the doll out to him.

He hesitated, not wanting to touch it. Not because it was evidence, although it probably would have been, had they not illegally tampered with the grave. Touching the doll would be a connection to the person who'd put it into the grave. That was a connection he would have liked to have avoided, but he could see that wasn't possible.

He took the doll, then reached for Karen. He just wanted to get the hell out of here. And fast.

"Look at this," Karen said after they'd left the cemetery far behind. The lights from Missoula bled through the low-hanging clouds making the buds on the trees glisten bright new green. It was the trees that made Missoula the Garden City. Soon the branches would be filled with lush green leaves that would form canopies over the streets.

Carefully, she held out the doll for him to see.

Someone had tied a piece of surgical hose around the doll's neck like—like an umbilical cord, Jack realized with a start. "Oh, my God," he whispered.

She put the doll down on her lap and stared at it. "It looks as if a child made the clothes for it." He could hear the emotion in her voice and knew she was close to tears. "I think this doll was Liz's."

His gaze leaped to her. "What makes you think *that?*"

She turned back the small collar on the doll's worn dress. The tiny homemade tag inside read: Jones Original.

"I had a doll just like this," she said. "Twenty years ago. That's when they came out. Every girl my age wanted one for Christmas that year. I got mine early, for my eighth birthday."

"I guess you're right," he said, not wanting the doll to be Liz's. Not wanting to believe she'd put it into the grave. Tangled a piece of hose around its neck, just as nature supposedly had done to her baby?

He didn't want to think about the person who'd buried the doll. Or about the real baby, Joanna Kay. Could this mean that she was still alive? He knew that was what Karen was hoping. But he wasn't so sure. None of this made much sense. Who in his right mind would bury a doll?

At the hospital, Denny had been given something to sleep and was out like a light, visiting hours were hours away and the nurse wouldn't let Jack and Karen stay.

Jack stopped by his apartment, just long enough to check the mail and answering machine. On the spur of the moment, he grabbed something for Karen and stuck it into his pocket.

Back in the Jeep, he noticed how exhausted she looked. She should have been convalescing. Not digging up graves. She looked so small and frail. It drew on every protective instinct in him. "I'm taking you home."

She smiled. "Home. I love the sound of that."

He smiled over at her, choked up by the rush of emotions she evoked in him. Just as impulsively as a few minutes before when he'd dug it out of the drawer in his apartment, he pulled the small velvet box from his jeans pocket. "With everything that's happened I forgot to give you this."

She stared down at the box, her eyes lighting up. He watched her take it, her fingers trembling, and for one moment he thought he'd only made matters worse.

But then she opened it, saw the thin worn gold band and said, "Oh, Jack."

"It was my grandmother's." That was all he could get out. He'd seen her glance at her naked ring finger. He didn't want her to think that her husband hadn't cared. Everything else might be a lie, but he did care. God, how he cared for this woman.

She slipped the ring on her finger. It was only a little loose on her slim finger. She looked up at him, love glowing in her eyes, the exhaustion and horror of the night washed away for the moment.

He couldn't have asked for anything more than that. He started the Jeep and drove toward the lodge. Home. He didn't care that it wasn't true. He blocked out the guilt and the voice that tried to warn him he was about to make the worst mistake of all.

Karen curled against him. He put his arm around her and pulled her close as they drove through what little was left of the night.

A COOL BREEZE sighed at the panes as Karen padded barefoot into the living room. She could see her husband silhouetted against the fading darkness beyond the front window. He stood motionless, his hands buried in his jeans pockets as he looked out. She stopped to stare at his broad shoulders, his strong back, the ache in her almost overwhelming to hold him. If only she could remember, then there would be no reason they couldn't make love. No reason he couldn't lie next to her and hold her in the darkness of the bedroom.

Or would there be? Why did she sense there was more to it than her injury and memory loss? That whatever was troubling Jack had something to do with her? With them?

"Darling?" she called softly.

He turned, his eyes hooded but she saw his reaction to her standing there in the long silk nightgown, the fabric falling over her curves, cupping and skimming, as sensual as any garment she'd ever owned. The perfect honeymoon attire. She'd purchased it earlier on the way to her shop for grave-digging tools. She'd run into a small boutique while Jack waited in the Jeep.

Now she realized the only thing that would make the gown more perfect was to have Jack take it off her. Slowly, lovingly. To feel his hands brush over the silk, over her expectant body.

"Karen," he said, his voice sounding hoarse.

She moved to him, joining him at the window. In the distance she could see Missoula's lights, twinkling like stars on a dark canvas of velvet black.

"Jack, I don't care what the doctor said," she whispered as she ran her hand along the top of his shoulder, down his arm to take his hand and press it to her heart. "I want you, Jack. I need you."

She heard his sharp intake of breath; she could feel the same vibration humming through him. She had never doubted that he wanted her. She knew he was just trying to protect her health, doing what the doctor had ordered. Only the doctor didn't know what was best for her. Jack was. She needed him. And now.

"Please, Jack. I can't bear spending another night in that bed alone."

SHE LOOKED LIKE an angel standing there in that long white gown. He'd never seen anything so beautiful. So sexy. So stirring. He could feel her gaze on him. A current ran through him, making him ache with need, filling him with a desire that threatened to drop him to his knees.

He ran a hand down her arm, over the silky fabric and drew back, telling himself all the reasons this was wrong. Then why did it feel so right?

He cupped her face in the palm of his hand and thumbed across her cheek to her lips. She turned her head to kiss the pad of his thumb as it skimmed over her cheek in a slow arc. He closed his eyes and groaned as she sucked his thumb into her mouth.

His eyes flew open. "Karen—"

She hushed him with her gaze and the slow shake of her head. As she stepped closer, his free hand cupped her slim waist, sliding to the small of her back.

She unbuttoned his shirt and slid it from his shoulders. It dropped to the floor. He slid his hand to her round firm buttock and pulled her to him. Silk against his bare skin, her breasts, heavy and firm, beneath it, pressed against him.

He dropped his mouth to hers. The kiss was hot and wet and when he pulled back, his body felt on fire. He let his gaze slide down her slim neck to the deep V of the gown. Rosy pink nubs of nipples pressed against the fabric, straining as if begging for his mouth. He turned her in his arms, kissing the back of her neck, telling himself all the reasons he couldn't do what his body demanded, pleaded he do. This side of her was just as tempting as the other, he realized belatedly as she pushed her wonderful round behind into him.

He heard her pleased chuckle as she confirmed that he wanted her as badly as she did him. She reached behind her to cup his jaw in her hand and turned with a dancer's grace to face him again.

And oh what a face she had. So sweet, her eyes liquid emotion, her lips full and soft and so inviting—

"I want to make love with you," she whispered.

"It's unbearable being this close to you and not touching, not kissing you, not—"

He could smell her scent as she moved closer, her body warm beneath the gown, the silk slick and cool against his skin. Her body molded to him. Then her lips. Pure sweetness. Just a little taste. Like a dusting of powdered sugar.

He knew he should stop her before she turned up the heat. Before he got caught in the fire between them and couldn't get out. But suddenly her kiss was pure sweet confectionery and he was warm taffy in her hands.

With a groan he pulled her even closer, kissing her as she had kissed him. Sweet and soft. Hard and hot. He'd never felt such desire. He'd never wanted a woman the way he wanted her.

She slipped a hand behind his head and drew him down to her breast. The nipple leaped at the touch of his tongue, straining against the thin fabric. He drew the rosy hard tip into his mouth and suckled gently. She moaned, her head back, the moonlight on her face.

"Jack, please, make love to me."

He looked down into her eyes and knew he was lost. He knew what he was about to do was far worse than digging up graves but he couldn't stop himself. He wanted her. He'd wanted her since the first time he'd seen her.

And he couldn't have turned back, even if he'd wanted to. For in that instant in time, he believed his own lie. He swept his wife up in his arms and carried her to their bedroom.

Chapter Fifteen

Jack woke in the early afternoon with Karen in his arms. He looked down at her incredible face and felt a tidal wave of emotion that threatened to drown him.

He lay for a moment trying to wade through those emotions. But one kept pulling him under. Guilt. It drowned out everything else, leaving him confused and afraid.

He'd made love to her, letting her believe they were married. Something he'd promised himself he wouldn't do. Couldn't do. And yet, he'd never wanted anyone more in his life.

To make his guilt worse, he didn't regret making love to her. How could he regret something so wonderful? He told himself it had been because he'd bought into his own lie. He'd truly felt "married" to her. He'd been caught up in that whole two becoming one thing. And it had been incredible.

But while he couldn't regret what they'd done, he couldn't forgive himself. Just as he knew Karen wouldn't be able to when her memory returned.

All told, he felt rotten. Was rotten. He feared he

had destroyed whatever they could have had together.

He tried not to think what that might have been or
how remarkable and rare it was as he slipped his
arms from around her.

She moaned softly in her sleep, the sound tugging
at him like an undertow. The strength of that pull
scared him. He already felt shaken from their lovemaking—and afraid. Afraid for Karen because of the
killer after her. Afraid of the hurt she'd feel when
she learned the truth about the man she thought was
her husband. Just afraid he would have to pay an
unbearable price for what he'd done. That price, he
feared, was losing Karen.

She moaned softly and flung an arm out as if
reaching for him. He stared down at the hand now
resting on his bare chest. The sparkle of his grandmother's wedding band gleaming like fool's gold. He
closed his eyes, the pain too much.

After a few moments, Karen seemed to fall into a
peaceful sleep again. He opened his eyes and gently
lifted her hand, trying desperately to ignore the sen-
sations her touch evoked in him as he slipped from
the bed.

He scooped up his hurriedly discarded clothing
and left the bedroom, leaving Karen in the big bed
they'd shared. Telling himself he didn't want to wake
her because she needed her sleep.

The truth was, he didn't want to face her this
morning. What would he say? He'd taken his lie too
far. He'd let himself become too involved with this
woman. Worse, he knew how this would end. He felt

a hard, cold ache of heartbreak, knowing that he'd just put the kiss of death on what could have been.

He wanted to confess, to make himself feel better. To end it now before he caused either of them more pain. But doing that would surely jeopardize Karen's life. That was the one thing he would not do.

He glanced at his watch, surprised to see how late it was. Early afternoon. Not that many hours before the third and final, he hoped, meeting with the third person who'd responded to Karen's ad. He had to concentrate on that right now.

He didn't believe for a moment that the meeting was anything more than a last-ditch attempt to draw Karen out and kill her. But he had a plan.

He picked up his cell phone and taking it outside, he made his first call.

"I have Karen Sutton," he said when Detective Captain Brad Baxter answered. "I'm bringing her to the third meeting."

Silence.

Jack hoped Baxter had a little cop in him. But even the politician in the man would want this case solved. And Baxter had to know, just as Karen had pointed out, that unless the killer believed she'd be there, he had no reason to show.

The best way to get the word out, considering that Jack suspected a leak in the police department, was to tell Baxter. He'd gear up for a worst-case scenario. Word would spread. The killer, hopefully, would hear that Karen would be there.

"If I see you I will have you arrested for obstructing justice," Baxter said without much force.

"Seems fair," Jack said and hung up.

Baxter hadn't threatened. Hadn't even raised his voice. But then he probably hadn't heard about the grave Jack and Karen had dug up last night. Yet. Nor did he know just how far Jack planned to go to get the killer.

Jack called Denny at the hospital next. "I'll be by soon. I just wanted to let you know that I'm taking Karen to the third meeting. It's the only way to draw out the killer and Karen insisted."

Denny chuckled. "Sure. Just don't try to sell me any Arizona oceanfront property, all right."

Jack knew Denny wouldn't believe it, but he'd had to try. And if he was dead wrong and Denny had killed Liz? Well, Denny was in the hospital, laid up. He was no threat to Karen.

Not that Jack could believe Denny had killed Liz. Or that he would harm Karen. But Denny had lied to him about a woman a few years back. It was that lie, like a tiny crack in a dike, that worried at Jack.

"You talked to Vandermullen?" Denny sounded anxious.

He didn't want to give his friend false hope. "There's a chance your daughter is still alive."

Denny let out a sound so filled with emotion that it tore at Jack's heart. "I'll tell you everything when I see you."

The third call was to the only man Jack trusted to leave with Karen.

KAREN WOKE TO THE EMPTY BED, Jack's side still warm, his imprint still visible in the mattress. She placed her hand on the spot where he'd been, remembering last night, relishing in it. Her body felt as if it glowed with an inner fire that Jack had ignited. It blazed still, warm and comforting even without him close by. She only wished she'd found herself in his arms this morning and they'd made love again, refueling that already burning fire.

So where was her husband? She sat up, wondering if he was in the kitchen making breakfast. She sniffed. No bacon frying. No sound coming from that direction.

Slipping from the bed, she pulled on his robe and went to find him. Immediately she realized he wasn't in the lodge. But through the front window, she could see him out by the rock wall with his cell phone pressed to his ear.

The danger he'd said she was in came back in a rush of secondhand memory. She knew just by the set of his broad shoulders that whatever he was doing had to do with the Liz Jones murder case. And her. Her husband wouldn't be able to rest until the killer was caught. She'd seen the worry in his eyes, felt the restlessness in him and sensed him holding back. Was he afraid to love her too much for fear of losing her?

But at least for a while she had made him forget the murder. Forget everything but the two of them. It had been heaven. She smiled at the memory of the hours they'd spent making love. For her, it had felt like the very first time with him. And amazingly, Jack seemed just as surprised by the wonder of it.

She couldn't believe how good they were together. How they had found each other and now had the kind of passion she'd only dreamed of. She'd known they had to have had a great sex life. She'd felt the chemistry between them and hadn't been able to wait to make love with him.

Oh, how she wanted to take her husband back to bed this morning. She opened the front door and padded barefoot out onto the small porch. After all, they were on their honeymoon, weren't they?

"Jack?" she called.

He turned and for an instant, she saw his love shining in those brown eyes, then he dropped that protective cover she'd seen before, mouthed a few words into the phone and pocketing the cell phone, walked toward her.

"I have some police business I need to take care of," he said before she could invite him back to bed. She could feel the distance he was trying so hard to put between them. But she could also feel him weakening at just the sight of her. As if he ached to touch her. She started to reach for him, knowing once they were in each other's arms—

But she didn't. "I'll get dressed and we can go," she said quickly and started back toward the bedroom.

"No," he said, making her spin back around to face him. "This is something I have to do alone."

"On our honeymoon?" she asked, her voice cracking. It wasn't that he was leaving her alone. It was the look in his eyes. The wall he was trying so hard to construct between them. Why? What was he so afraid of? It couldn't be them, their marriage. Not after last night.

"I have to be at the last meeting today," he said. "I have to find the killer, Karen."

Before he finds you. He didn't say the words, but she heard them in his look.

She nodded. He was just trying to protect her. Nothing was wrong between them. She forced herself to smile. "I know you're doing it for me."

He nodded. "Are you hungry? I could make you some breakfast before I leave."

She would have liked that. But it wasn't food she wanted. She wanted Jack and it was clear he was anxious to be on his way. "No, you go on and get your business finished. I can manage." She saw him hesitate. He really didn't want to leave her. "I was hoping to explore the chalet today, anyway."

That seemed to do the trick. He smiled then, knowing how much she loved the old things Crazy Uncle Chuck had collected, and stepped to her, planting a quick kiss on her forehead. "I'm not leaving you alone. I called—"

"Jack, I don't need a baby-sitter," she said, touched by his concern but not wanting a stranger around. The truth was, it made her feel more vulnerable. "I feel safe here and no one even knows about this place, right?"

He nodded and smiled. "I know I'm probably being a little overprotective—"

"A little?" she asked, raising a brow, glad to see some of the worry fade in his gaze, some of the reinforcements come down from the wall between them. "Have you told Denny about the baby yet?"

"I'm stopping by there," he said. "I just hate to get his hopes up, you know?"

She knew. For a moment, their gazes met, but Jack pulled away, stepped away. *Let him finish this case,* she told herself. *Let him realize nothing is going to happen to you. You'll always be with him. Always.*

In the distance she could hear the whine of an engine as a vehicle climbed the mountain toward them.

"I'm going to go, then," he said, sounding relieved.

"Tell your friend to make himself at home," she said, not wanting to deal with company. She needed to be alone with her thoughts today. She wanted to think only about their lovemaking. Only about the love she'd seen in Jack's eyes.

The chalet would be the perfect place to spend the rest of the afternoon. It was like finding lost treasure, all the wonderful old things. In them she felt a connection with the past. A solid foundation as if each generation built something for the next. Like the cabinetry she constructed. Something that would last.

"I'll be back as soon as I can," Jack said, obviously distracted as he headed for his Jeep.

"Be careful," she called after him. "I love you, Jack."

He didn't turn around. Maybe he hadn't heard her.

She stared after him, his broad shoulders, the muscled back, his long legs, all so familiar now. How she ached to hold her husband and not let him go.

For just an instant, she felt such a terrible sense of foreboding she wanted desperately to call him back. It was such an odd feeling. She told herself being married to a cop she had to get used to him being in dangerous situations. But she knew it was more than that. This feeling that she might never see him again, that something would happen while he was gone that would separate them forever felt like a warning, an omen.

She shook it off. When had she started believing in premonitions? But she would have called Jack back. Would have begged him not to go—if she'd thought he would have listened. If she thought he could have stayed with her.

But a part of her knew her husband. Knew he had to go. Until the killer was caught, Jack Adams wasn't going to let himself love her. Not the way her heart promised her that he wanted to.

So she watched him leave and prayed the killer would be caught soon. She needed her husband. And Jack needed her. Maybe he just didn't realize how much yet.

JACK DROVE AWAY, sick inside. "I love you, Jack." Her last words echoed in his head, in his heart, filling him with guilt and shame. He'd done things he wasn't necessarily proud of, but he'd never been a coward. Or a liar. Or a thief.

He'd stolen her heart in the most despicable way, destined to break it. *Let her memory come back,* he prayed. *Let her remember the killer before it's too late.* Karen's safety was all that mattered. Even if it meant losing her.

He told himself he couldn't think about any of that now. He had to catch the killer. Stop him before he got to Karen. Jack drove to the hospital, determined to put an end to all the lies tonight when he returned to the lodge and Karen, no matter what happened today. He couldn't take any more. He couldn't lie to her anymore.

Denny looked better, but still weak. Still vulnerable. Jack knew it had more to do with worrying about his daughter than the physical effects of his injury.

"I can't believe you dug up the grave," Denny said, sounding impressed rather than horrified. "That was something like what I would do."

It was true. Denny had always been the hothead, the one in trouble. So why was Jack now about to lose his job, his career? He still couldn't understand what it was between him and Baxter, some animosity he'd never understood.

"Once we saw that someone had already started digging—"

"You're kidding," Denny said. "Did you see who it was?"

Jack shook his head and told Denny about the person who'd taken a shot at them. "Someone didn't want us to know that the only thing in that casket was a doll."

"A doll?" Denny asked in surprise.

"Karen thinks it was Liz's from when she was a girl."

Denny's eyes widened slightly, his jaw tightened. "Vandermullen."

"He had to be in on it," Jack agreed. "But Liz must have agreed to go along with the plan to give up the baby for adoption. She wouldn't have been looking for your daughter if she hadn't known about it, right?"

"But why?" Denny asked, sounding in pain. "Why didn't she tell me about the baby? Why did she give her up?"

Jack shook his head. "Maybe Vandermullen knew

it wasn't his kid and put pressure on her. Who knows?''

Denny nodded thoughtfully. ''You think she was killed because she was searching for our baby? This mystery man. If he took the baby, maybe he didn't want Liz finding out where our daughter is.''

Jack shrugged. It was a possibility. But at this point, only speculation. For all they knew the baby might not even be alive. But like Denny and Karen, Jack was starting to believe she was. And that Liz's death was tied to the illegal adoption.

''So, you're going to try to draw out the killer tonight,'' Denny said.

He nodded. ''I'm worried that if this really is about your daughter, then we've uncovered enough that the killer is feeling trapped. I'm afraid of what he'll do.''

''He probably figures he has nothing to lose now,'' Denny said in agreement. ''That he's going down one way or the other. But he plans to take Karen with him. A last-ditch effort to eliminate the eyewitness.''

''And maybe a little payback,'' Jack said, scared Karen had a deadly enemy out there who wasn't going to stop until he killed her.

''That makes Vandermullen a prime suspect.''

''And the man who took Liz's baby,'' Jack said. Who knew how far that man would go to keep the girl's identity and whereabouts a secret? How far he'd already gone? ''For all we know, the mystery man and Vandermullen may be in this together.''

Denny seemed lost in thought. When he looked up, his gaze softened. ''How's Karen?''

Jack shrugged noncommittally. He'd seen the hurt in her eyes this morning and knew she must be confused. He wished with all his heart that he could erase parts of the past, the way the blow to Karen's head had erased part of hers. But mostly he wished he could erase the lie between them.

"I'm afraid I'm going to lose her. But not to a killer," Jack said vehemently.

THE THIRD MEETING was set in the park at the south side of the Clark Fork River. Denny had passed along Jack's idea for the female undercover cop to take Karen's place.

Jack watched with binoculars. Because it was a beautiful late afternoon, the park was full of joggers, sunbathers, dog walkers and bikers. What a terrible place for a stakeout. He kept his eye out for anyone who looked suspicious—a ridiculous task—and for other cops. Baxter especially.

Jack didn't expect anything to happen. The killer wouldn't show. He'd know the woman waiting on the park bench wasn't Karen.

But, Jack hoped, the killer would have to get close enough to be sure.

Half an hour went by but still no one had come near the Karen look-alike.

Then Jack saw the female cop grab her left shoulder and slump over. At the same time, cops who resembled sunbathers, dog walkers and bikers moved in.

Jack rushed to his Jeep and turned to the frequency the stakeout team was using. The female cop wasn't hurt badly from a gunshot wound. But an ambulance had been called. Had anyone seen the shooter?

Jack looked up and saw a car pull out on the other side of the river. It was a large, dark-colored American-made car and its driver seemed to be in a hurry.

He started the Jeep and without siren and lights, took off after it. The car was so plain. So nondescript. Just like detectives used for undercover work.

He raced across the bridge and down a side street, hoping to cut off the vehicle, but it had disappeared as if into thin air. Jack suspected the car and driver were sitting in a dark garage somewhere. Safe.

JACK DROVE TO the hospital, wanting to talk to Denny about the car he'd seen, the suspicions he couldn't keep to himself any longer. He couldn't be sure it was a cop car. Couldn't be sure of anything, including that the driver had fired the shot. Nor could he not listen to his instincts. But he needed Denny to bounce them off. He and Denny often did that at the bar after work. Right now, Jack needed his friend to tell him he wasn't crazy.

But when Jack reached the hospital, the nurse informed him that Denny Kirkpatrick had checked himself out without telling anyone.

"Was he well enough to do that?" Jack asked, surprised.

"No," the nurse said. "I hope he isn't driving. That could be very dangerous with his injury. But maybe his female visitor drove him."

"Female visitor?" Big surprise. Even laid up in bed close to death Denny could attract women. "Do you happen to know who the woman was?"

The nurse smiled. "As a matter of fact, I recognized her from the photo in the newspaper." She saw that Jack didn't know what she was talking about. "The one from Saturday's feature page. About a sweet sixteen birthday party at the carousel."

Sweet sixteen. The same age as Denny's daughter. "The woman was in the photograph?"

The nurse nodded. "With her daughter."

"Do you still have that newspaper around?" Jack asked.

She reached behind the desk and pulled out a battered copy of the *Missoulian*.

Jack quickly thumbed through it, stopping abruptly at the smiling faces of mother and daughter on brightly painted wooden carousel horses.

"Annette Westbrook?" Jack asked, his blood ringing in his ears. Baxter's sister. He'd met her once at some party when Baxter had first taken over as captain.

His instincts had been right! All his suspicions confirmed. Baxter!

But what made Jack's heart threaten to bust out of his chest was the girl with Annette in the photograph. Danielle Westbrook, sixteen, was the spitting image of Liz Jones except for her hair and her eyes. Both were dark—just like Denny's.

Chapter Sixteen

Jack found Detective Captain Brad Baxter at his home on North Street near the University of Montana. Baxter seemed surprised to see Jack. Or maybe it was the weapon Jack held. A police special. Denny's.

"You can't threaten me. I know my rights," Baxter said.

Jack laughed as he shoved the pistol into Baxter's face and backed him into the living room. "Did you think I was here to arrest you? Have you forgotten? I'm not a cop. You suspended me. Threatened to have me thrown in jail. I'm just here as an interested citizen who's going to kick your hide if I don't get some answers."

Baxter glanced toward the phone.

"Want to call the cops? Go ahead. But it really isn't necessary. They're already on their way."

He seemed to hesitate, probably thinking Jack was bluffing. "What makes you think I'll tell you anything?"

It was all Jack could do not to grab the man by his collar and slam him against the wall. But he wanted answers more than he wanted vengeance. Although that could change, if he found out Baxter had been the one who'd tried to kill Karen.

"Because," Jack said between gritted teeth. "I think you're a lot of things, Baxter, but not stupid."

His look of apprehension gave Jack guilty pleasure as Jack motioned for him to take a seat. He saw Baxter glance toward the coffee table, but head for a chair away from it.

The gesture made Jack suspicious, which was his nature, God knew.

Jack stepped closer, his pulse a hammer. On the coffee table was a county map. A red line on the map had been drawn from Missoula to Jack's ski lodge. Directly to Karen.

He looked up at Baxter, fighting an urge to harm the man. But no matter what Baxter had said or done, Jack *was* a cop and he didn't believe in taking justice into his own hands. Lucky for Baxter.

"I'm worried about Karen Sutton," Baxter said, obviously seeing the murderous glint in Jack's eyes. "I figured you had her hidden up there. I just wanted to make sure she was safe."

So Baxter knew about Jack's inheritance. How many other people did?

"You're the man she saw with Liz at the Carlton, aren't you," Jack said, finally voicing his suspicions. "You killed Liz Jones."

He lowered his head into his hands. "She was alive when I left her."

Jack stared at Baxter's bowed head, the pieces starting to fall into a pattern that, while didn't necessarily make sense, fit.

"My God," Jack cried. "Is that why you put me on probation when you did? You knew you were going to have to kill Liz and you wanted me out of the way?"

Baxter glanced up, that old condescension back in his eyes. "Are you so arrogant that you'd think I put you on probation because I was afraid you'd solve this case if I didn't?"

Baxter must have realized the irony of it. Jack had solved the case. Or had he? Was this where it all ended? Or did he just want to believe the worst about Brad Baxter?

"Then why did you put me on probation?" he demanded. "Why now?"

Baxter looked away. "It doesn't matter."

"Like hell. Damn you, Baxter, I know your sister has Liz's daughter. I know you're involved with Vandermullen. You were trying to protect him. You killed Liz to keep her from finding out that your sister Annette Westbrook had her baby."

Baxter wagged his head. "I didn't know the baby was Liz Vandermullen's. I thought I was getting a baby that an unwed teenaged girl didn't want."

Jack shot him a look of disbelief.

"My sister always wanted a baby, even when she was a little girl. It's all she wanted. When she found out she couldn't have children, she was devastated."

"She could have adopted legally," Jack suggested sarcastically.

"She has health problems that made her a poor candidate for adoption."

"So you decided to get her a baby any way you could."

"I heard about a doctor who sometimes helped put the infants of unwed mothers with families for a fee."

"Dr. Vandermullen."

Baxter nodded. "He said he had one that would be available in February or March. I had no idea it was Vandermullen's own child."

Did he really not know the baby was Denny's?

"He got me all the paperwork, making it appear that Annette and her husband were the parents."

"So Danielle doesn't even know she's adopted?"

Baxter nodded, looking more miserable. "Annette thought the baby came from an unwed teenager, just like I did. I hadn't known until last week that Liz had been told her baby died. Nor that she hadn't been able to have more children."

That was news to Jack. "Then she didn't want to give up the baby for adoption?"

Baxter shook his head sadly. "She found out that Vandermullen had drugged her and lied about the baby being born with its umbilical cord wrapped about its neck. He'd also done something to ensure that she'd never have any other children when he delivered the baby that night."

Jack shuddered. "The sick bastard." He must have realized it wasn't his kid. That's why he'd buried the doll in the grave with the cord around its neck. He'd wanted to hurt Liz. He'd sterilized her. He'd wanted to hurt the baby, but he hadn't. Why? Because he could sell it and punish Liz even more by him knowing that her baby was alive and she didn't know it?

"So why didn't she go after her ex?" Jack asked. "She must have wanted to kill the bastard."

"She wanted to find her baby more than she wanted to get even with her husband, ex-husband," Baxter corrected. "I think she was afraid of him."

With good reason.

"That's probably why she told Karen Sutton what she did," Baxter said. "Except Karen thought Liz meant she'd found a secret lover through the personals."

"Instead, she found you," Jack said, seeing how Karen had been misled. Liz must have been afraid to tell Karen about the baby. Even to the end, she must have been trying to protect her and Denny's baby. "She found you and she ended up dead. Coincidence?"

"You're looking in the wrong place," Baxter said. "Liz told me she thought Vandermullen had been following her. I didn't take it seriously because I had…tailed her a few times. I saw her the day she met with Karen at the coffee shop."

No wonder Baxter had looked so surprised to see Karen at the Carlton the night Liz was murdered. It hadn't been the wine stain at all. He'd seen her before. With Liz. His confession only made Jack more sure he'd killed Liz.

"Then Liz *did* come back to Missoula looking for her daughter?" Jack said.

"She'd remembered seeing me that night with the baby but it had all been like a dream because of the drugs. She came looking for me after she'd somehow learned that the baby really hadn't died. She put the ad in the paper."

"So why didn't you just not answer it? Ignore it?"

"I don't read the personals, but my sister Annette noticed it and called, thinking it odd that it was the same day as Danielle's birthday. I knew the moment I saw the ad. I guess I've always feared something would come of the…adoption. I knew Liz would find me eventually. See my picture in the paper or see me on the street. I thought if I met with her and explained—"

"So you met with her, secretly," Jack said.

"She wanted to know about her daughter. I told her Danielle was with a good loving family, had a wonderful life and that she didn't know she was adopted. I begged Liz to leave it alone because of all the lives she'd ruin if it came out. I knew what it would do to Annette and Danielle."

"But you couldn't convince her." So you killed her.

"That's just it, I *did* convince her."

"Then why did she call Karen and say she'd found out everything and was demanding answers the night she was murdered?"

"She saw a photograph in the newspaper of Danielle's sixteenth birthday," Baxter said with a groan.

The same one Jack had seen. Just a wild shot a photographer had taken at Danielle's birthday party at the city carousel. Like him, Liz must have recognized her daughter. It didn't take much to figure out that Annette Baxter Westbrook was Captain Baxter's sister.

"This time she wasn't so easy to convince," Jack said, starting to see the whole picture. "So you had no choice but to kill her."

Baxter looked away for a moment. "Do you want to hear the truth or not? You seem to have already made up your mind that I'm guilty."

Jack had always thought of himself as a good cop. A fair cop. Baxter hit a chord. "All right."

"I asked her to give me time to tell Annette so I could prepare her and Danielle. I promised to call Liz the next day and let her know when she could meet her daughter. But I never got the chance before the call came about the murder."

Jack shook his head. "It's a little too neat. With Liz dead, your secret should have died with her. Except for Karen. You couldn't be sure that Liz hadn't told Karen about you and Vandermullen and the child the two of you stole from her."

"You don't believe me," Baxter said simply.

"No. You put Karen in a safe house only to have it blow up. How do you explain that?"

He shook his head. "I can't. The killer found out somehow."

"Right. What about the second stakeout? You pulled everyone off when you saw Karen near the carousel, realizing you'd missed killing her at the hotel."

"I called them over to the hotel because I thought Karen was inside," Baxter said angrily. "How was I to know she'd tricked the officers guarding her?"

He could have found out from those same officers that Karen had gotten away. Baxter would have surmised that she'd head for the second stakeout, as stubborn as she'd proven to be about helping solve the murder.

''Did you know that Danielle's father wasn't Vandermullen?'' Jack asked.

From Baxter's shocked expression Jack figured he really hadn't known. ''Then who—?''

''Denny Kirkpatrick is the father,'' Jack said, enjoying Baxter's shock.

''No, my God,'' Baxter said, taking it even harder than Jack had expected. He knew there was no love lost between Baxter and Denny but the captain looked more than shocked. He looked…sick. ''I just didn't want my sister and Danielle hurt.''

Jack stared at him. Was there something more to this?

''Didn't you realize that killing Liz would hurt them?''

''I'm a cop,'' Baxter said quietly. ''I've made mistakes trying to protect my family, but I'm not a murderer. Why do you think I've told you all this? You think you have your killer and that this woman you care about is safe. You're wrong, Jack. The killer is still out there and will kill Karen Sutton if you foolishly think this is over.''

''Then who does that leave?'' Jack asked.

''Vandermullen,'' Baxter said without hesitation.

Suddenly he was no longer trying to protect the good doctor. ''With your testimony, Vandermullen will be picked up,'' Jack assured him. Just not for Liz Jones's murder. Not without proof. Nor would Baxter go to prison for Liz's murder without proof.

And Baxter knew it. Karen was the only one who could put Baxter at the hotel that night with Liz. That might be enough for a jury to convict him. But without Karen—

"There is one other person—" Baxter hesitated, his face contorted in pain. "My sister, Annette." He sounded close to tears. "That's why I got the map to your lodge, Jack. I'm afraid she might have killed Liz. That she might harm Karen."

Jack stared at him. Would Baxter stoop so low as to finger his own sister for murder just to save himself?

"She was at the hotel that night," he said, looking upset about what he was saying. "I saw her. She was very distraught. I tried to talk to her—"

Jack recalled that Karen said she saw a friend of her mother's at the hotel that night—just down the hallway from Liz's room. Could it have been Annette Westbrook? His blood ran cold. What if he *was* wrong? What if Baxter wasn't the killer? "Could she have found out that Liz was looking for Danielle?" he asked.

"Maybe."

Jack told himself that Baxter was just trying to shift the blame. To confuse him. To make him second-guess himself. But he couldn't shake the thought that the killer might still be loose. Still out there.

Baxter looked up, almost in surprise, at the sound of a siren.

"You're under arrest," Jack said as he opened the front door to let the police officers in.

"Please read him his rights," Jack said to one of the officers.

Detective Captain Brad Baxter sat quietly. Jack waited until the officers had cuffed and loaded Baxter into the back of a patrol car.

Then certain that at least he wouldn't have to

worry about Baxter, Jack climbed in his Jeep, anxious to get back to the lodge and Karen. But he had one stop he had to make first. Because his gut instinct told him he had to be sure he'd just had the right man arrested.

THIS EARLY in the afternoon on a nice spring day, Dr. Carl Vandermullen wasn't in his office, just as Jack had guessed. But he was at the golf course. Jack found him in the clubhouse, drinking bourbon on the rocks.

"You son of a—" Jack jerked Vandermullen to his feet by his polo shirt. The other two golfers at the table with the doctor started to get to their feet and come to Vandermullen's defense. "Don't even think about it," Jack snarled.

"It's a personal matter," Dr. Vandermullen said quietly as he motioned for his golfing buddies to leave them alone. He freed himself from Jack's hold. He was stronger than Jack thought he'd be. "Perhaps we could discuss this in one of the private dining rooms?"

Jack followed him into a quaint little room that looked out on the course and a stand of aspens. Along with a half dozen tables and twice that many chairs, it was furnished with a sitting area, complete with love seats and a bar.

"Care for a drink?" Vandermullen asked as if this were a social call.

Jack knew he had to keep his cool. The last thing he wanted to do was get arrested. He had to get back to the lodge and Karen. But he had to judge for himself if what Baxter had told him was the truth.

"I'll pass on the drink," he said between gritted teeth. "You lied about the baby."

Vandermullen poured himself a bourbon and sloshed it around, the ice clinking softly on the glass. "I had to."

"The same way you had to lie about drugging her, stealing her baby, selling it and pretending it had died?" Jack asked angrily.

Vandermullen stared at him. "What are you talking about?"

"Brad Baxter told me everything. How you drugged Liz, sold him the baby and then lied about it being born with the umbilical cord around its neck."

The doctor shook his head. Either he was a great actor or—

"Liz was the one who wanted to give up the baby. Not me. I wanted a child. I knew I couldn't have any of my own." He nodded at Jack's surprise. "I'm sterile."

Jack frowned. "Then you knew Liz was carrying another man's baby?"

"Johnny K's."

This wasn't going anything like Jack had thought. "What about the grave, the stone, the doll—"

"Liz's idea. It was rather her way of saying goodbye to the baby. She put one of her dolls in the grave with a cord around its neck." The doctor made an unpleasant face. "I thought it was…morbid. But she insisted. She didn't want anyone to know. Especially Johnny K. I guess you know him as Denny Kirkpatrick. She wanted the past put behind her. That's another reason she insisted I sterilize her."

Jack felt weak. "You're telling me that was her idea?"

"She knew I couldn't have children so I think it was her way of putting us on equal footing."

Jack raised a brow. Did Vandermullen really expect him to believe this?

"You didn't know my wife. She was quite... neurotic."

Jack was having a hard time believing this and yet the doctor seemed to be telling the truth. "Then why was she suddenly looking for her baby?"

Vandermullen shrugged and took a drink of his bourbon. "It's hard to say. Maybe after all these years and our breakup, she needed an anchor. Someone to love. It happens. It's too bad. She would have destroyed whatever family Brad Baxter found for the baby. Liz was a very needy woman, as I've told you. She would have brought no good to her daughter."

"If you feel that strongly," Jack said carefully, "would you have tried to stop her?"

Dr. Vandermullen smiled. "As I told you, I washed my hands of Liz. And I certainly wouldn't have committed murder to protect a baby that wasn't even mine."

"But you did perform an illegal adoption, fake a baby's death and lie about it," Jack pointed out.

Vandermullen didn't even flinch. "I would have done anything for Liz. Whether you believe me or not, I loved my wife, detective. Sadly, I still do." He glanced at his watch. "Tee time."

Vandermullen left him to go golf with his friends, leaving Jack confused. He didn't know what to believe. Vandermullen had had an answer for everything. He'd also seemed pretty calm when he'd headed off to collect his clubs and hit nine holes before dark.

Jack was just glad Baxter was behind bars and Karen was safe, because it appeared that Baxter was a consummate liar and more than likely a killer.

Jack couldn't wait to get back to the lodge and Karen. He'd decided one thing for sure. He would tell her the truth. How he'd lied about their marriage. But everything else had been real. Something *had* happened to him the moment he saw her. He just hadn't known what it was. He thought he knew now. But did he know what he wanted to do about those feelings if Karen gave him the chance? Right now, he was still running scared. Afraid that somehow he'd missed something...

The police radio filled with a burst of static, making him jump. He reached to turn it off but didn't get the chance before he heard the bulletin.

Detective Captain Brad Baxter had escaped after being arrested at his home.

Jack swore. Karen! He turned on his siren and, with lights flashing, sped toward the lodge, praying he'd reach her in time.

Chapter Seventeen

Karen heard a noise, almost like the sound of a vehicle, and realized that hours had passed. She brushed dust and cobwebs from her shirt and glanced at her watch. Maybe it was Jack returning. She hoped so. She really wanted to talk to him. To try to get him to open up to her. Something was bothering him and she suspected it was more than this case.

She knew she couldn't keep pretending that nothing was wrong with their marriage. She'd hoped that once they made love again, it would change the worried look in Jack's eyes. She'd thought it must have something to do with her fall in the phone booth. What an odd place to fall down. It still puzzled her what they'd been doing there. Maybe she'd been calling her mother.

Jack had insisted she not call her mother and tell her the news of their marriage until after Karen's memory returned and she was no longer in danger. He didn't want to worry her mother. She'd thought that sweet. But she couldn't help but wonder if Jack had her hid away up here because of Liz's murder and a killer being after her. Or some other reason.

He was definitely hiding something from her. She knew him too well. Especially for as little time as she could remember knowing him. She'd never felt such a connection before. A closeness. As corny as it sounded, a oneness that she'd never believed possible with another human being, not even through marriage.

So what was Jack hiding from her?

SHE OPENED the chalet door and peered out. There was no vehicle by the lodge. Not even a car belonging to the man Jack had left to take care of her.

Suddenly she felt guilty. She hadn't even said hello to Jack's friend who'd been kind enough to drive all the way up here to look after her. Maybe she could make them both some coffee.

"Hello?" she called as she walked in the path cut for the chairlift down toward the ski lodge. The chairs dangled overhead, black silhouettes like stick figures against the evening sky.

She realized she hadn't even thought to ask Jack's friend's name. And felt guilty. Jack was only trying to protect her. Why had she gotten her back up about that? Because she didn't want to be dependent. Hadn't that always been her fear? That marriage would take away her independence?

As she came around the corner of the lodge, she saw the thunderheads. Rain. She could smell it on the air.

"Hello?" Still no answer. Maybe he was inside. "Not much of a guard, Jack," she said to herself and laughed.

She pushed open the door to the lodge, suddenly

aware of the silence. It felt thick as cotton and just as dense. "Hello?" she called more softly.

No answer. She hadn't really expected him to be in the lodge, she thought, trying to reassure herself that everything was fine.

But as she walked back toward the door she saw something on the coffee table that stopped her. The confidential police file on Liz Jones.

Karen was positive it hadn't been there earlier. Jack had left his cell phone on the coffee table but she would have noticed the file if it had been there.

With morbid curiosity, she pulled out the contents. One of the photos of Liz caught her attention before she had a chance to look at anything else. The photo, taken after her death, showed the panty hose tied around Liz's neck.

"Oh, my God," Karen whispered. Her heart rate quickened. She stared at the photo, an icy blade of understanding burying itself inside her.

The panty hose. The cord around the baby's neck. Why hadn't she noticed the similarities? The killer had wrapped the panty hose around Liz's neck the same way someone had the cord around the doll's neck in the grave.

Karen shoved the papers and photograph back into the file and pushed it under a stack of magazines, feeling dirty, as if she'd glimpsed inside the killer's dark, sick mind.

She shivered. The lodge suddenly seemed too quiet. She hurried out on the porch into the last of the day's sunshine.

As she stood on the porch and looked out, she wondered about the vehicle she thought she'd heard earlier. She'd so hoped it was Jack returning. But she heard nothing now. And nothing moved on what she could see of the winding road that dropped off the mountain. Either she'd been mistaken or...was it possible her "guard" had left for some reason? That could explain why his car wasn't here and why she'd thought she heard a vehicle and why he didn't answer.

Silence seemed to shroud the mountainside. It was the storm, Karen told herself. And what she had seen in the file. What she suspected.

"Hello?" she called again, her voice echoing back at her and nothing more. "Fine," she said, losing interest fast in continuing to look for her guard. He'd probably left. Or maybe he'd parked on the road below and walked up this morning. And now he could be out scouting around the perimeter or sleeping in the shade of a tree or a— She glanced down at the stone wall below the lodge. Or sleeping in the shade of a wall.

Shoes. She could see shoes. Black penny loafers. Jack had left her in the care of a man who wore penny loafers? And white socks, she saw as she moved closer. She could see his ankles now. Pant legs. Slacks? *Geez, Jack, who did you leave guarding me?* Certainly not Bruno the Biker. But just the sight of him, reassured her.

She continued down the steep hill until she could see a shirt over the top of the wall. Striped. It matched the slacks. It appeared Jack's friend cared more about clothing than Jack did.

With relief she stepped up onto the wall, looked down and saw the man sleeping in the late sunshine, a fedora over his face and him completely unaware of the approaching storm or anything else.

JACK RACED toward the ski lodge. He couldn't believe Baxter had escaped and had a good head start. Jack tried to convince himself that Baxter would run. A cop with his background would know how to disappear.

But Baxter wasn't going to disappear. Jack knew where he was headed. The ski hill and Karen. Baxter knew where she was and how to get there. He'd just resisted arrest. He'd know he wasn't going to get away with what he'd done. The best he could do would be to get even. Did he blame Karen? Or did he think that by killing the eyewitness to Liz's murder he might still be able to get off somehow?

Baxter didn't know that Karen couldn't remember anything after he'd hit her in the phone booth. Karen couldn't identify him. He was safe. The irony of it made Jack weak. Karen might never remember.

But worse than all that, she wouldn't know that Baxter was the killer when she saw him. She would be a sitting duck.

His fear growing, Jack hurriedly dialed the cell phone number at the lodge. He had to warn her. The phone rang and rang. No answer. She was in the chalet. He'd left the cell phone on the coffee table in the lodge. She wasn't answering because she didn't have the phone. She was safe still, though. Baxter hadn't had time to get to the lodge. Yet.

It began to rain, huge drops that splattered loudly on the windshield like pebbles.

KAREN STOOD on the rock wall, debating whether to let her "guard" sleep or not. It would be cruel to let him get caught in the storm, although he definitely deserved it. Falling asleep on the job. Good thing she didn't *need* help.

She jumped down from the wall with a thud she thought would wake him. But he didn't move. A lot of good he'd do her. He hadn't heard her calling for him, he hadn't heard—

She froze. Blood. It was matted in his hair just over his ear. Reluctantly, she leaned down and carefully pushed the hat back from his face. She leaped back, a shriek escaping her lips. Her heart thundered in her chest.

"Howie?" she cried, not even realizing for a moment that her memory had returned at the sight of him.

She dropped beside him and searched for a pulse. Weak, but he was alive. But what was he doing *here*, she wondered as she stood. Surely he couldn't be the guard that Jack had—

Jack. Her memory filled in like a flooded hole, drowning her in the truth. She grabbed hold of the stone wall as memories tumbled down on her. One truth lodged itself in her heart, a splinter of unbearable pain.

Jack. Her mind searched frantically for any other explanation—but found none. Jack. He wasn't her husband. He'd lied. She thought of their lovemaking and closed her eyes in agony. He'd pretended to be her husband. He'd pretended to love her.

She opened her eyes, struggling against the anguish with the only weapon she possessed. Anger.

What a fool she'd been. How could she have believed they'd gotten married so quickly? That she'd fallen in love with him almost at first sight?

But you had *fallen in love with him. And almost at first sight.*

And Jack must have known that. He'd used it against her. Used it to "protect" her. How could he have done such a thing to her?

She looked down at Howie. The only thing that mattered right now was getting help for him. He must have fallen.

She spotted a rock a few feet away—stained with blood. Her heart rocketed. He hadn't fallen. Couldn't have fallen on the rock. It was too far from him. She'd only been kidding herself that everything was fine. Nothing was fine. Jack had lied to her. And a killer was after her. How could things get any worse?

She knew the answer to that as she looked toward the lodge. The silence now absolute. Something rumbled behind her making her jump. Just the thunder as the storm moved closer. Rain imminent.

Trying to act as if she still believed Howie had just suffered a bad fall, she headed for the lodge. And the cell phone. Call for help. Call Jack. Just the thought of hearing his voice—

She'd call the police. Not Jack. Soon enough she'd have to face Jack. Face the fact that it had all been a lie. And that she knew he'd betrayed her love. Betrayed her.

She reached the lodge, hurriedly locking the door behind her. The cell phone wasn't on the coffee table where Jack had left it that morning. Where she had just seen it minutes ago. She glanced around the lodge, trying to remember if she'd moved it. Her head was reeling. The phone *had* been on the coffee table.

"Are you looking for this?" a voice asked behind her.

JACK RACED THE JEEP up the mountain but hadn't gone far when he came around a bend and saw a car blocking the road. He stared, his headlights slicing through the rain, that now fell hard and fast.

Denny's car?

Jack couldn't believe what he was seeing. What was Denny doing here? Why would he check himself out of the hospital to come up here? Especially in his condition and knowing Jack wouldn't be here?

Jack stopped behind the car, his headlights cutting through the empty interior of the car. Fear clutched at him, colder than the rain hammering the Jeep's roof. How had Denny found the ski lodge? If Baxter had figured it out, then Jack supposed anyone determined enough could.

Including the killer.

He tried the cell phone again, praying that Karen would answer. At least she wasn't alone. He'd left his cousin Howard with her. The line rang and rang.

He got out of the Jeep and walked toward Denny's car, wondering why he'd stopped in the middle of the road. To block it for anyone else coming up behind him?

Just as Jack suspected, there were no keys in the car, nor was he able to push it out of the way.

Where was Denny? What could have made him

leave the hospital in his shape to drive all the way out here?

Jack knew he'd have to go the rest of the way on foot. But so would anyone behind him. He took off at a run up the steep mountainside, following the winding road, fighting back the fear and panic that he'd reach the lodge too late.

KAREN STARED at her mother's bridge club member and the gun in the woman's hand, wondering crazily what her mother would have to say about this. "Annette?"

Annette Westbrook was small, with blue eyes, blond hair and the slight figure of a mere girl. It seemed so odd to see Annette with a gun. The other times, Annette had cards or a wineglass in her manicured hand. The gun looked completely out of place.

The cell phone in the woman's other hand finally quit ringing. Had it been Jack calling to check on Karen? Annette acted as if she hadn't even heard it. She seemed a little dazed.

"You know, don't you?" Annette said after the heavy silence filled the lodge again. "You remembered everything, didn't you?"

Annette had known about her memory loss? "I don't know what you're talking about," she said edging back toward the fireplace—and the poker, telling herself this wasn't happening. None of this was happening. Let it all be a bad dream. Especially the part about Jack not being her husband.

It was the pistol Annette held that convinced Karen this wasn't a dream and kept her from even considering trying to overpower the woman. "What's going on?"

"I need you to tell me something," Annette said, her voice deceptively soft, gentle. With her free hand she reached into her purse.

Karen couldn't have guessed what the woman would pull out even if she'd been given clues.

Annette withdrew a silver frame and offered it to her the way she might have an appetizer.

Karen stopped inching her way toward the fireplace to take the nicely framed photograph. As she glanced down at it, she was surprised to see that it was of Annette, a man she'd never seen before and a beautiful young girl who looked familiar and another man. It was that man, the one on the far right, who grabbed Karen's attention.

"You recognize him, don't you?" Annette asked with a strange politeness, considering she was holding a weapon on her. "He's the man you saw with Liz Jones, isn't he?"

Karen looked up, knowing her surprised expression had given her away. "Who is he?"

"My brother, Detective Captain Brad Baxter."

Karen couldn't hide her shock. Jack's boss. The man she'd seen in the Hotel Carlton hallway with Liz was Jack's boss? No wonder he'd been in the hotel ballroom that next morning. He'd returned to the scene of the crime all right—returned to pretend to investigate it.

She stared down at Brad Baxter's photo and realized what it was about him that caused her to recognize him as the same man she'd seen only briefly before. His ears. They were good-sized and stood out from his head in a way that she hadn't realized made him very recognizable. Even in silhouette.

"Where is he?" Annette asked as she took the photograph back.

She looked up at her. "Where is who?"

"My brother."

Karen slipped closer to the fireplace. "I have no idea." She bumped into the stone with her heel.

"He isn't here?" Annette glanced around nervously and Karen took that moment of distraction to reach behind her and feel for the poker.

"Why would he be *here?*" Karen asked and darted a look toward the bedroom.

It worked. Annette followed her gaze in that direction, giving Karen the opening she needed. She gripped the poker firmly and swung. It was only a glancing blow, but enough to knock Annette out. Her eyes rolled back and she slumped, the gun and cell phone clattering to the floor next to her.

Karen held the poker, waiting to see if the woman moved. When Annette didn't, Karen exchanged the poker for the gun and cell phone.

Holding the gun on her, hands trembling, Karen punched in 911. Thunder boomed overhead. Rain pounded at the window. It took her a moment to realize that the number wasn't ringing. She tried again without any luck. The tower must have gone down in the storm.

She looked down at Annette, not knowing what to do. For the life of her, she couldn't imagine Annette killing Liz. Or clobbering Howie with a rock. But then, before a few minutes ago, she couldn't have imagined the woman holding a gun on her, either.

Annette still hadn't moved, but Karen couldn't trust that the woman wouldn't come to soon. Tossing the cell phone aside, Karen pulled down the cord from the drapes and tied Annette's hands and feet, keeping the gun nearby just in case.

When she'd finished, Karen noticed the gun. She stared in disbelief. It wasn't loaded. Why had Annette come all the way up here to threaten her with an empty gun?

Something hit the window. She looked up startled. Raindrops began to beat against the glass. Wind rattled the panes as the sky darkened and thunder rumbled off in the distance.

For a moment, Karen stood frozen, afraid to move, too confused to know what to do if she did move.

She'd have to get Howie help. She had to get them both out of here. Now. Annette would have driven. Her car must be just down the road. Karen fished through the contents of Annette's purse. No car keys. Then checked Annette's pockets. She must have left the keys in the car.

She checked to make sure Annette's feet and hands were still bound tightly enough, then started for the door, wondering what had made the woman think her brother would be here?

Karen opened the front door hesitantly, not sure who or what she'd find outside waiting for her. The sky had turned a bruised and angry blue-black. Rain dropped in a torrent. She could see her breath but little else through the cloudburst. It was now or never.

As she stepped off the porch, she ran toward the road as if the bogeyman were after her. For all she knew, he was.

OUT OF BREATH and drenched from the rain, Jack slowed as he neared his cousin Howard's black sports car parked beside the road. Howard hadn't driven all the way up the mountain. Not that Jack could blame him. The road only got worse closer to the lodge and Howard drove one of those expensive two-seaters. Jack realized that Howard had probably been lucky to get this far.

Jack had passed him that morning farther down the road, assuring himself that Howard was the perfect person to leave with Karen. His cousin had a black belt in karate, although you'd never know it based on his chosen profession—floral design.

As Jack drew closer to Howard's car, he saw something that escalated his already rocking fear. All four of the tires had been flattened.

Jack started past the car at a run again. Ahead he could see that there was another vehicle parked up the road. He didn't recognize it and realized Baxter would have ditched the cop car for something less conspicuous.

Jack had only gone a few yards when he heard a sound off to his right. He turned, but not quickly enough. Something hard and cold struck his temple. He saw a flash, like fireworks, then nothing. His last memory was hitting the ground, hard.

THE MOMENT KAREN SAW the red four-wheel-drive car parked a short way from the lodge, hidden in the trees, she knew it had to be Annette's. She raced to it, jerked open the door and leaped in, locking the door behind her.

Rain pounded at the glass, blurring everything beyond the windows. She reached around the steering column for the keys. They weren't in the ignition.

She stared, uncomprehending. If Annette didn't have the keys on her, and they weren't in her purse or the ignition... She spotted them in the little tray in the console and clawed them out, fighting tears.

She could fall apart later. Not now. Not yet. Shaking from the cold and the fear and the relief, she got the right key into the ignition. The car started. She closed her eyes for an instant in silent thanks. Everything was going to be all right now. As long as she didn't think about Jack and the pain that came with it. As long as she didn't think that there was a killer still after her.

She shifted into gear, determined to drive this rig up as close to Howie as she could. She knew it wouldn't be easy to load his dead weight— Bad choice of words. He was still alive. He had to be.

She pulled up to the end of the wall, then bracing herself against the cold, slipped out, leaving the engine running, and hurried along the wall to where she'd left Howie, still wondering how she'd get him into the car.

It wasn't something she was going to have to worry about.

Howie was gone.

"Howie!" she shouted, glancing around for him. The rain must have revived him. Would he head for the lodge?

She looked toward the lodge, then back at the spot

where she'd found him lying. The rock that had had the blood on it was still there. A few feet away, she saw Howie's hat, rain-drenched and lying in a puddle. On past it, she saw the drag marks. Heel prints in the mud.

Her gaze followed the marks up the mountain, stopping on the one black loafer, lying on its side in the rain.

Oh, God. She felt her legs turn to water. Her head swam as she realized what she was seeing. Someone had dragged Howie's body up the mountainside. It couldn't have been Annette. She wasn't strong enough.

Karen turned and felt as if she were running in quicksand. The car. If she could just reach it. She could get out of here and get help.

She reached the car again, jerked open the door and threw herself in, using the power lock to lock all four doors.

For a moment, she didn't move, just sat breathing hard. Rain pounded on the roof like a steel drum and the thunder moved closer, louder, more ominous. Maybe that was why she didn't realize at first that something had changed.

The car engine was no longer running. She reached to start it again.

The keys were gone.

Chapter Eighteen

Karen sat perfectly straight, not moving, not breathing, fighting the panic that had her heart ready to burst from her chest.

He was behind her.

In the back seat.

She could hear him breathing. Just like she'd heard him breathing on the phone when he'd called her number, after he'd killed Liz Jones.

She fought the urge to look in the rearview mirror. To face her killer. To face her fate.

She forced her gaze down to her hands. They lay in her lap, shaking. She knew she'd never reach the door handle, throw the door open and get out before he grabbed her.

He was playing with her. He could have killed her several times over. He wanted to make her suffer first. Just as he was doing right now. Waiting. Watching her. Enjoying her pain. Tasting her fear.

Anger numbed the fear. She let only her gaze shift away from her lap to the console between the plush seats. Something glittered between the seat and console in the dull light. She saw that it was one of those anti-car-theft devices, a foot-long metal rod.

She took a breath, knowing he was waiting for her to try to escape. He would be anticipating it. But she knew he would never let her get out of the car. If he could help it.

She began to cry softly, finding the tears more easily than she would have liked. He'd like tears. She would give him that—if it bought her the few precious seconds she needed.

Her hand dropped over the cold steel rod at the same time she glanced in the rearview mirror. All she saw was his head, covered in the hood of a dark-colored sweatshirt—and his eyes looking out of the cloaked darkness.

The moment she saw the glitter of the malevolence in his gaze, she knew this was what he'd really been waiting for. He wanted to see her terror when she saw him, when she realized he was right behind her, waiting to kill her.

His arms came over the seat for her. Just as his hands grasped for her, she clutched the metal bar, and swinging her right arm back through the space between the seats, drove the end into his ribs as hard as she could, catching him by surprise. He let out an *Umfph!*

She struck him again. Harder. She felt the steel connect solidly with his ribs, heard a sharp loud crack and a satisfying cry of pain. He recoiled, the dark shadow of his arms above her retreating. Temporarily.

She unlocked her door and threw it open, then hurled herself out into the rain again. She landed on her hands and knees. Scrambled to her feet and ran blindly down the road, the steel bar still in her hand. She wanted to keep running and never look back. But it was miles to the nearest paved road. Miles to the nearest house.

She slowed, fighting panic. Think, Karen. Think. She stopped running and spun around, raising the rod to strike, expecting to find the killer right behind her.

All she saw was rain and the stormy darkness as she stared back up the mountain. The driver's side door was still ajar, the overhead light shining through the rain. The car appeared empty.

She heard a branch break below her down the mountain. She listened. Another crack. Someone was just below her on the road.

She turned and ran back toward the lodge, remembering something she'd seen in the chalet farther up the mountain. An old double-barreled shotgun and a half-empty box of shells.

She worked her way through the trees and the rain, watching for movement. Where was he? Still in the car? Somehow she doubted that. Just like she doubted he would just leave now. Leave her alone. He couldn't do that, could he?

The thunder drowned out any sound she made. But it also made it impossible for her to hear someone sneaking up on her.

She reached the side of the chalet and stood back against the rough rock, trying to catch her breath. Through the rain she thought she saw something move near the ski lodge. She stared until her eyes ached but saw nothing.

Hurriedly, she slipped around the building and into

the dark chalet. She didn't dare turn on a light and give herself away.

She felt around, her fingers falling on the cold steel of the shotgun. She clutched it to her breast and felt for the shells.

Six left. She stuffed four in her pocket. Breaking the shotgun open over her thigh, she pushed the remaining two shells into the old double-barrel and snapped it shut.

She took a breath, held it as she listened for any sounds beside the drumming of the rain on the chalet roof. She debated waiting here for him, letting him come to her. There were places she could hide in the chalet. But for how long?

Suddenly the sound of the generator filled the air. A light came on high in the rafters of the chalet, spilling down on her. Exposing her. Making her an easy target.

He was right here with her.

She spun around, raising the shotgun, afraid she wouldn't be able to get a shot off in time before he was on her.

Nothing moved. Nothing, because, she remembered belatedly, when an outside light was turned on at the lodge on the mountain below her, this one came on in the chalet.

She lowered the shotgun and hunkered against the wall for a moment, trying to chase down her heart. She knew she'd have to either do something about the light or take her chances outside in the dark.

She had no idea where the light switch might be nor did she have time to look for it. Hurriedly, she looked around for something small and heavy, and spied a can with an assortment of large rusted bolts. Setting down the shotgun reluctantly, she hefted one of the larger bolts and taking aim, threw it at the naked lightbulb in the rafters.

The bolt missed, showering her with dust and dirt. She picked up another bolt, this one larger. Calmly. A confirmed tomboy like herself should be able to do this. She threw. The lightbulb shattered, showering her covered head with broken glass this time— and blessed darkness.

He'd see the light go out and know where she was. But she'd have a much better chance in the dark. And no matter where she hid, he was going to come looking for her. She didn't try to fool herself about that.

She picked up the shotgun again, deciding she would stay in the chalet and wait for him.

But then she heard something over the storm and the thump of the gas generator. The strange chilling sound of metal scraping against metal. It took her a moment to realize what it was.

The chairlift. He'd started it up. She could see the shadow of a chair inching slowly past the dirty chalet window in the rain.

Why had he started the chairlift? The lift ran from below the lodge up the mountainside, right past the chalet where the chairs dropped low enough that skiers would have been able to get off—or continue on up the mountain to the top.

Was he riding the lift up the mountain to her? Why? Had she hurt him that badly? Or was this just another way to torment her?

He didn't know she had a weapon. Maybe he *would* be arrogant enough to ride the lift to her.

Cautiously, she opened the door and stepped out into the rain. The chairlift groaned even louder out here. She stared at it, surprised it still worked.

The chairs rocked with the snail's pace motion, dark against the storm. She could see them creeping up the mountain, headed for her.

Another bolt of lightning eerily illuminated the string of chairs. With a start, she saw that one of the chairs coming up the mountain had someone on it. Just as she'd expected. He was riding right to her.

Her first instinct was to run. But how far would she get before he jumped off and came after her? Worse yet, he would be able to see from up there. He'd know where she'd gone. It was just a matter of time before she'd have to face him.

She stayed in the shadow of the chalet and waited for the dark figure on the chairlift to come to her.

She was shaking so hard, she wasn't sure she would be able to pull the trigger, let alone hit him. She made a swipe at her eyes with her sleeve. *Get control. Get tough. Think about Jack.* But along with her anger at Jack came a terrible sadness that was almost her undoing. It wasn't bad enough that the man she loved had lied and betrayed her. She was about to face a killer. Alone.

She brushed at the tears that mixed with the rain, knowing she couldn't give in to her pain. She stared at the figure through the rain. He sat on the chair that inched toward her, one leg propped up against the far side of the chair, the other dangling down. Casual. As if he didn't have a worry in the world.

She stayed in the shadow of the building, not

wanting to give herself away. Not yet. Wait until he saw the shotgun. Wait until she pulled the trigger.

He didn't move on the chair. Just kept coming, slowly, ever so slowly, the chair grinding almost in pain as it creaked closer and closer.

It was almost to her when she stepped directly into the chair's path, lifting the shotgun, ready to fire.

Lightning splintered the sky in a burst of blinding light that cracked like a gunshot.

Karen flinched, her finger on the trigger, as she focused on the figure riding the chairlift. Ready to fire.

But in that instant of intense light she saw something that changed everything. White crew socks illuminated in that burst of storm energy. White socks. And one black penny loafer.

The killer came at her from behind, his breath ragged as if he'd run up the mountain. But there was no weakness to the arm he clamped around her neck, imprisoning her in a headlock. Strong. Unforgiving. She stumbled, the shotgun slipping from her hands and sliding down the mountainside into the rain and darkness as she reached up to claw at his arm.

An animal cry tore from his throat, almost a cheer. He had her. She wasn't getting away. Not again.

"You just couldn't leave it alone, could you?" he demanded in a fierce hoarse whisper. "You have destroyed me. Ruined my life. Hunted me down like a dog. Now you're going to die."

JACK CAME UP out of the blackness of unconsciousness. His head ached. He pushed himself up on all fours, the rain running down into his eyes. Rain and blood, he realized, as he touched his head and his fingers came away sticky.

Karen. He stumbled to his feet, his vision blurring for a moment as he fought to keep upright. He felt light-headed. Off balance. And strangely naked.

He felt under his arm, against his ribs. The holster was empty. The gun gone.

THE CHAIRLIFT continued to groan, the chair with Howie in it rocking as it moved toward Karen and the killer.

She could see Howie now, his face pale, his body slumped in the seat, one leg up against the far side of the chair, the other with the one missing black loafer dangling lifelessly as the chair inched nearer.

Karen realized the chair with Howie on it would hit her and the killer if they didn't move.

Close to her ear, she heard the killer chuckle as she fought to free herself from his hold, but even as she tore at his sweatshirt jacketed arm and his face with her hands and kicked back at him, she knew her efforts were wasted. He was too strong for her. Too determined to kill her.

He tightened his hold, cutting off her air. She couldn't breathe. Couldn't speak. Blinded by the rain and her own tears, she thought of Jack. She wanted him to be her last thought. Her best thought. It didn't matter now that he didn't love her. She loved him. And it was all she had now.

Lightning splintered the sky like a flashbulb going off in her face. Thunder came on its heels, earsplittingly loud. In that fraction of a second, she saw him. And she knew he'd seen her. Miraculously, Jack was coming up the mountainside as if her love for him had made him appear.

But at the same time, she realized he'd never be able to reach her in time. Darkness was closing in. She needed air. Desperately.

She struggled, knowing the man behind her was enjoying making her suffer. He wouldn't let her die easily—or quickly. She hoped.

Howie's chair was almost to them. The killer seemed to realize that they were about to be hit if they didn't move.

Just as he started to drag her back, she lunged for Howie. Wrapping her arms around his shoeless leg, she pulled with every ounce of strength left in her.

Howie's inert body didn't budge, as if he were bolted down to the chair, and for one heart-stopping moment, Karen thought her last-ditch effort had been wasted.

Her vision narrowed to only a pinpoint of light. Her lungs cried out for air as she teetered close to passing out. The arm around her neck tightened as the killer tried to pull her back, but she held tight to Howie's leg, the chair rocking.

Then when she didn't think she could hold on any longer, she felt Howie's body give a little. He came crashing down on her, breaking the killer's hold on her as they all three fell to the wet ground.

Karen heard the swinging chair hit something with a thud. The killer let out a curse. She fought for air, the darkness refusing to relent to the light. She could hear her attacker struggling nearby. As her vision began to clear, she could see two figures, limbs entangled. Air filled her lungs and she sucked in huge gulps.

As her attacker tried to free himself of Howie's inert body, he groaned and she realized she *had* injured him earlier in the car. He was holding his ribs.

She tried to get to her feet, gasping for breath, her throat on fire. His hood still shadowed his face as he finally managed to throw Howie off and lunge through the pouring rain for her.

She scrambled to get away from him. But she didn't move fast enough or far enough. He caught her ankle and dragged her toward him. She kicked furiously at him, hoping to connect with his injured ribs.

Suddenly Jack appeared behind the killer. She saw him lift the chunk of wood in his hands and bring it down. The killer's grip on her ankle loosened as the wood struck him in the shoulder, but he didn't go down. He shoved Karen out of the way as he turned to launch himself at Jack.

She fell back, tumbling and sliding down the hill, finally coming to rest against a tree stump. Above her the two wrestled beneath the chairlift. She scrambled back up on hands and knees toward them.

She didn't hear the chair behind her. Forgot about it until it hit her, flattening her to the ground.

She lay dazed for a moment, then looked up to see it inching toward Jack and the killer. The chair struck one of them in the back. She watched in horror as the corner of the chair seemed to catch on a piece of his clothing, dragging the man along as he fought to free himself.

It wasn't until the chairlift rose, the ground falling

away again beneath the chair, that she saw the man dangling helplessly wasn't Jack.

The figure hanging from the chair wore a sweat-shirt. It was the hood that had hung up on the chair. He now clung to the chair with one hand. The other cradling his ribs as he tried to tear his hood loose.

She watched in silent horror as the man's efforts failed and he finally dropped his arm. The chair jerked along with him hanging by his neck, his arms at his side.

The body continued on up the mountain. She watched. Time suspended. The chair came through the bullpen and headed back down, slowly, painfully.

She saw Jack get to his feet. The rain began to lessen. In the dull light of the passing storm and the approaching night, she stood a few feet from him, the two of them just looking at each other. Jack Adams. More of a stranger than he'd been before her memory loss.

A cop. A man who went around saving damsels in distress. That's why he'd pretended to be married to her. Why he'd pretended to love her. Just to keep her safe. To protect her. That's what cops did.

And he *had* saved her. If only he'd saved her from this heartache, as well.

She stood in the drizzling rain and cried as over-head the sound of a helicopter drowned out the gas generator and the grind of the chairlift. A spotlight splashed down from the chopper as it hovered above her.

She dragged her gaze away from Jack and looked up at the corpse hanging from the chairlift as the chair crept closer.

The spotlight shone on Dr. Carl Vandermullen's face as he dangled lifelessly against the passing storm clouds.

KAREN'S MEMORY had returned. Jack saw it in her eyes. In the silent accusation there. In the hurt and betrayal.

But it was the pain in her gaze that was his undoing. His heart broke. Snapped like a twig. Leaving only an unbearable ache that tore at his insides.

He knew his pain was nothing compared to hers. She looked more devastated by what he'd done than by her encounter with a killer.

He'd destroyed the best thing that had ever happened to him. Why would she ever trust him again? He'd used her love and trust to fool her. All in the name of protecting her. It wasn't enough that he'd lied about the marriage. He'd bought into it himself.

He felt weak as he stumbled toward her, searching for words that would take away the pain. His Girl Next Door. God, what had he done?

Below them on the mountain, he saw Denny. He had Baxter. Baxter's hands were cuffed behind him. Annette stood nearby.

Chapter Nineteen

The hours that followed, passed in a blur of pain and confusion. Paramedics and police. A rush of uniforms and questions. So many questions.

Jack had tried to talk to her, to comfort her, but she couldn't bear to look at him, couldn't bear to hear his explanations.

"Jack, I understand," she'd said. "You were just trying to protect me." That's what cops do.

"Karen, there is so much I need to say to you."

But she hadn't let him. She'd felt too fragile. Too afraid she'd shatter if he touched her. Break into a million pieces if he told her it had all been a lie. Even the love she thought she still glimpsed in his eyes. Just looking at him hurt too much.

Jack was flown out with Howie and Denny for medical treatment, his chief insisting he go. Karen could tell that Jack didn't want to leave her, as if he still felt responsible for her—the last thing she wanted.

Later, when she reached Missoula, she'd called the hospital just to make sure he was all right. They were keeping him overnight for observation.

She went to her mother's. Jack phoned. She didn't take his calls. When he stopped by to check on her, her mother turned him away at her request.

She couldn't bear to see him. Nor hear his apologies. Or witness his guilt. It was easier to believe the lie he'd told her than reality. As crazy as it seemed, she still thought of him as her husband. She would always remember what it had felt like in his arms. Making love to him. And ache for him.

She knew in time she would convince her heart that it hadn't been real. But right now, it was just better if she didn't see him.

Between the newspapers, her mother's grapevine and Howie's and Denny's visits, Karen put all the pieces of Liz Jones's death together over the days that followed.

Dr. Carl Vandermullen was dead, but he'd left a signed confession at his home, detailing why he'd killed Liz. He'd never forgiven her for being pregnant with another man's baby. She'd told him it was his child, not realizing he was sterile. He'd played along, disposing of the baby—and making sure Liz never had any others.

When she'd found out what he'd done, she'd divorced him and gone looking for her baby. He'd killed her to keep her from exposing him. But he'd also killed her because he just couldn't let go.

As Denny had said, the clues had been there all along. The panty hose around Liz's neck. The cord about the doll's neck. Vandermullen's fabrication of how the baby had died.

Liz's search for her lost child had set off a string of events that had led to her death—and had almost gotten Karen killed because of a chance meeting on a street corner.

Karen's mother was shocked, of course. Karen didn't tell her about Jack. Or the fake marriage. Or her heartbreak. She didn't have to.

Pamela Sutton was glad when no charges were brought against Annette Westbrook and the bridge club didn't have to look for another member. Karen figured Annette had just been trying to protect her brother and had never meant her any harm.

Denny finally admitted that the woman he'd been seeing on the sly was Annette Baxter Westbrook. They'd met one night when he'd gotten a police call about a prowler in her neighborhood. Annette had been separated from her husband at the time and later divorced.

Baxter had found out about Denny and Annette. He'd threatened Denny and finally used Jack as leverage to try to keep Denny away from his sister. That's why Baxter had put Jack on probation—to make Denny back off.

Denny had, for Jack's sake.

Detective Captain Brad Baxter confessed to a long list of wrongdoing, including the hit-and-run attempt to scare Karen at El Topo and the assault in the phone booth near the carousel. He also admitted using his position on the force to coerce Denny and Jack and giving Vandermullen Karen's location at the safe house.

He said he'd had no choice. Vandermullen had been blackmailing him, threatening to take Danielle from his sister. He'd done what he had to protect his sister and his ''adopted'' niece. Baxter swore he'd

escaped custody, though, to go to the ski lodge to try
to keep Vandermullen from killing Karen. His trial
was set for later in the fall.

The best news was that Denny had met his daughter and he and Danielle had hit it off. Annette and
Denny were seeing each other again, taking it slowly.

Danielle had always suspected she was adopted.
She seemed relieved to have found herself in Denny,
as if discovering a missing piece of a puzzle.

Jack was off suspension and he and Denny were
going to get commendations. Karen was glad Jack
hadn't lost his job. He was a good cop. Just the kind
of man any woman would want protecting her.

Aunt Talley sent goodies with Howie for her. All
her favorites. Too bad baked goods didn't cure a broken heart. Then brownies, fried pies and cinnamon
rolls would be the perfect food.

True to form, Howie and his aunt tried to fix her
up with his cousin J.T., her perfect match. But she'd
sworn off blind dates, even if she hadn't figured out
that J.T. was Jack Thomas Adams.

She'd hoped that as the days passed she'd get over
the heartache. Her mother and Denny and even
Howie and Aunt Talley convinced her that work
would be the best thing for her. Finally one morning
late in March, she headed for her shop. She'd been
avoiding the shop, knowing that Jack's ghost would
be everywhere she looked.

She hadn't gone but a few blocks when she heard
the siren and looked in her rearview mirror to see
the flashing red-and-blue lights.

She was in no mood for a speeding ticket. In no
mood for a cop. She didn't recognize the car behind

her. Not a Jeep. Not this time. For a moment, she thought about not stopping. But she'd tried that once before and look where it had gotten her.

She stopped, unable to forget the last time she'd been pulled over. She heard the tap on the glass next to her. As she rolled down her window with one hand, she dug in her purse with the other for her license.

"May I see your license and registration, please," a very male voice asked.

She turned, the license in her hand, to stare at the man standing beside her car. "Jack." Dazed, she handed him her license, still reaching for the registration.

"I'm sorry, but you're going to have to step out of the car."

She turned to look at him. "What is this about?"

"You and me," he said, making her remember when he'd been hers.

"Please don't do this, Jack."

"Would you step out of the car, please," he said, sounding like a cop. Not the man she thought was her husband. He was wearing a worn hockey jersey, jeans and a baseball cap. She felt as if she'd been shot back in time.

"Jack, I know why you did what you did. It was just to protect me and I'm grateful—"

"I don't want your gratitude. Out of the car, please." Nothing showed in his face.

She opened the door and climbed out. "Jack, please—"

"Turn around and put your hands on the car." In

the shade of his cap, his brown eyes were dark, serious.

She did as he ordered, unable to stop remembering. Unable to forget the last time he'd frisked her. Only this time, she was wearing a bra. But her nipples reacted anyway, remembering his touch, anticipating it.

She closed her eyes, feeling herself weaken before he even touched her. "Is this really necessary?"

"Yes," he said quietly.

She trembled as his hand brushed over her hair, dropping to her shoulder. Tenderly. Tears welled in her eyes. Her body ached for him. "Don't do this, Jack." His hand moved down her back. Slowly. Lovingly.

"What are you afraid of, Karen? Remembering what we have together?"

"Had, Jack. Had."

"No, Karen," he said, turning her around to face him. "Still have. Will always have." He pulled her into his arms and kissed her.

She resisted at first, but even as she fought it, she felt herself melting into his arms, losing herself in his kiss. That old unlikely chemistry was still there, stronger than ever.

But chemistry wasn't enough. Didn't he realize that?

"What is it you want from me?" she cried, tears choking off her words as she pulled away from him.

"I've been miserable." His gaze said that was true. But was it because of his guilt or— "I love you, Karen."

Why hadn't she noticed that he'd never used those

words when they were "married?" How could she have been such a fool? "You don't have to say that just to—"

"To what, Karen? To make myself feel better? Do you really think that's all this is? That nothing that happened between us matters?"

"Jack—"

"No, you haven't let me tell you how I feel. I love you. We belong together. Yes, I made a very big mistake trying to protect you with a lie. But the marriage was the only thing that wasn't real."

She closed her eyes, afraid to believe him, afraid to trust her heart to him again.

"Karen, look at me," he said, his voice breaking. "Look into my heart. Then, if you still don't believe me…"

She opened her eyes and stared into his face, that wonderful boyish face. For days she'd told herself that the love she'd seen in his eyes before had all been part of the deception. She'd been hurt. Betrayed. Afraid to believe anything he said. But especially to believe the love in his eyes.

"Oh, Jack." She saw in his eyes what her heart had only dreamed of. "Oh, Jack."

HE LAUGHED, his heart soaring, and swept her up into his arms. "I think that means you believe me."

"Oh, Jack."

He kissed her again, promising himself he'd never let her go.

It had been Aunt Talley's idea. She'd plied him with her homemade gingersnaps. "You know I can't resist your cookies," he'd said. She'd smiled. "Yes, dear, I know.'' Then she'd proceeded to tell him how to get Karen back.

Amazingly, Karen's mother had gone along with the plan to get Karen out of the house and into his arms.

He'd hoped that if he and Karen touched, that bond would still be there. That if his words couldn't convince her, then maybe his lips could.

''I love you, Karen. I've loved you since the first moment I laid eyes on you. It just happened so fast that I didn't even believe it myself.''

''But you believe it now?'' she asked.

He smiled down at her. ''Oh, yeah. I want to marry you. The right way this time. Your mother, my family, the white dress, the church, the bridesmaids. I might even be able to talk Denny into being my best man.''

''Oh, Jack, I'd marry you at city hall.''

He shook his head, not about to miss seeing this woman walk down the aisle to him.

''I wouldn't have it any other way,'' he said as he pulled her closer. He wanted a real wedding for his Girl Next Door. And a real marriage. Complete with the babies he couldn't wait to start. ''Let's go break it to your mother.''

HARLEQUIN®

I N T R I G U E®

43 Light St.

Outside, it looks like a
charming old building
near the Baltimore
waterfront, but inside
lurks danger...
and romance.

"First lady of suspense"
Ruth Glick writing as
Rebecca York returns with

#558 NEVER TOO LATE
March 2000

Scott O'Donnell had believed he'd been betrayed
by Mariana Reyes, yet he still was unable to resist
the attraction that had consumed him six years
ago. Their reunion was laced with secrets and
danger. With a killer on their trail, Scott had to
protect Mariana—and the daughter he never
knew he had.

Available at your favorite retail outlet.

HARLEQUIN®
Makes any time special ™